I0712431

# *Horse Girl*

A novel authored by

Amaia Joy and Geoffrey Carroll

Publisher

Joyce E Jones

Publish by

Joyce E Jones

12 Chapel Lane

Tijeras, NM 87059

www.amaiaandgeoffrey.com


ISBN: 979-8-218-36634-6 (sc)


Illustrations, cover and interior by author

Geoffrey Carroll

# Eight million horses, donkeys, and mules died in War War-I

# NEW MEXICO

Utah
Colorado
Raton
Chama
Farmington
Taos
Santa Fe
Gallup
Albuquerque
Tucumcari
Santa Rosa
Rio Grande River
Socorro
Arizona
Roswell
Mimbres
Silver city
Alamogordo
Deming
Las Cruces
Carlsbad
Camp Cody
Columbus
El Paso
To San Antonio, Tx by train 500 m
Texas
Mexico

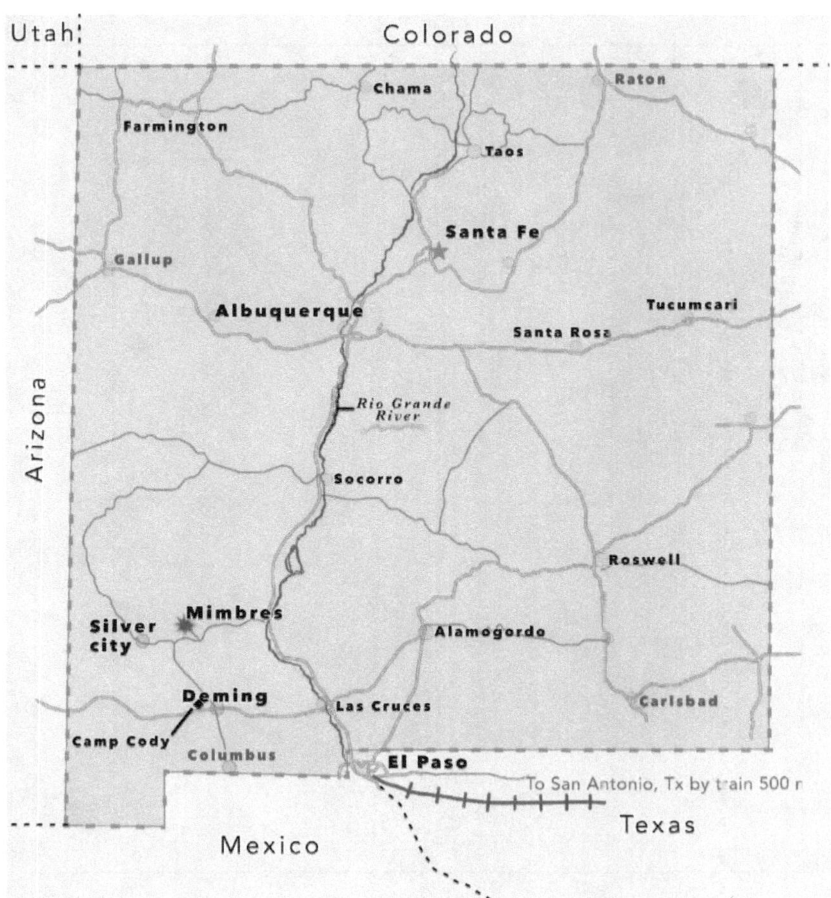

# FRANCE

England
Belgium
Calais
Fromelles
English Channel
La Havre
Fort
Champagne
Reims
PARIS
Nancy
Marne River
Best
Orleans
Dijon
Germany
Saint-Nazaire
Bay of
Bisqay
Lyon
Grenoble
Italy
Bordeaux
Nice
Montpellier
Toulouse
Marseille
Mediterranean

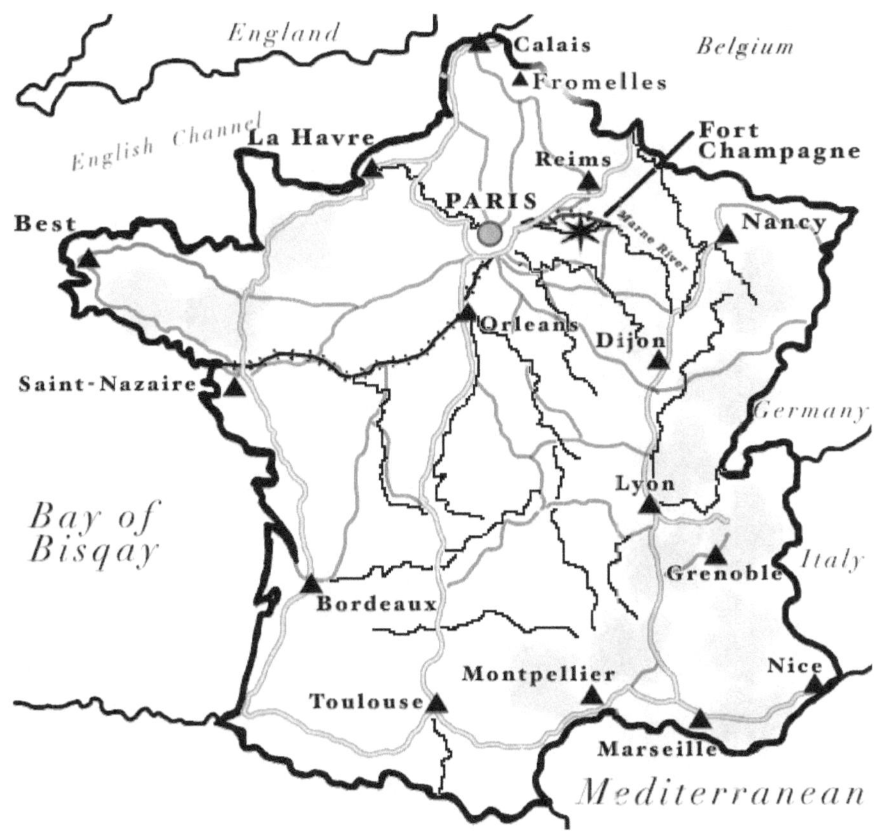

*The horse is made ready for the day of battle, but victory rests with the Lord"*

*Proverbs     21:31*

# Chapter 1

Spencer Penrose sat in his opulent red leather office chair, puffing on the cigar he had just lit—then leaning over with another lit match for Colonel Cambridge's unlit cigar. Both puffed laboriously to get their cheroot started. They sat back in their chairs, grunting, and puffing to get a good flame ablaze, cigar smoke bellowing into the increasingly smoke-filled office.

Swirling his overpriced Buffalo Trace Kentucky whiskey in his glass, Spencer interrupted his laborious puffing to take a sip, then continued their ongoing conversation. "I tell you, Alexander, that scrawny little Horse Girl can work miracles with any horse she gets her skinny little red hands on." Coughing, then clearing his throat, he continued in amazement. "It's a peculiar phenomenon, it's like… she somehow communicates with them."

Colonel Cambridge barked out proudly, "With the United States Army joining the fight in The Great War in

Europe and my cavalry headed to the Western Front next week, the US Army sure could use someone like that. It's just too damn bad, that she's a blathering woman and a red skin Indian too." Prejudice spilled from his words.

Spencer jumped to his feet as his words exploded, "I'll tell you what is too damn bad, is that she's married to my son, Junior." Rubbing his plumb fingers franticly over the top of his bald head, gasping for air, he breathlessly bellowed his vulgarity, "Son of a gun! My son is a fiddleheaded, bamboozled lunk. Damn that boy for thinking with his dick when he married that… that… that… Horse Girl."

There was a knock on his office door. Spencer's face, still red from rage, he swung open the door. He barked sternly, "What is it, Mr. Parker?"

Timidly, the Office Clerk spoke, "Mr. Penrose, Sir." Fumbling his words, he continued, "You wanted me to let you know when Miss Atencio was here to work with the company horses."

# Chapter 2

Mazie Atencio was born April 14th, 1887. She was the firstborn child of Ignacio Atencio and Anna Bidu. Anna was born and raised in Mimbres, in the New Mexico territory. As a baby, the first word out of Mazie's mouth was "caballo", which quickly became her world.

Mazie's father Ignacio, was a quiet and spiritual man with a talent for happiness. Born in 1868 to a Spanish family who immigrated to the New Mexico Territory to work in the Santa Rita Copper Mine. At the age of thirteen, he too, started working in the mine. At that time, the copper from the mine was excavated from caves, where the miners spent all day, six days a week, confined in the filth, dust, and soot.

Ignacio and Anna were only teenagers when they met while on a hunting trip in the Black Range Mountains. Their hearts quickly merged when they discovered they shared beliefs and spiritual interests. Although Ignacio was raised with Catholicism and held true faith in Christ, as an adult he never followed that religious path, nor did he encourage his children to do the same. He and Anna felt a soulful connection with God and God's source.

Centered in the beautiful Mimbres Valley, they built their homesteaded near the crystal-clear water of the Mimbres River. Their home was made from adobe bricks and pine vega logs in the tradition of Anna's ancestors.

The word "Mimbres" in Spanish means "willows." Their residence sat among the natural pine, pinion, cottonwood, and willow trees. Year-by-year, they developed additional irrigation ditches from the river, and year by year, they added more fruit trees of apple, pear, cherry, apricot, and plum, slowly becoming a rewarding orchard.

Ignacio worked at the Copper mine when work was available, yet together, Ignacio and Anna worked as equals to cook, clean, hunt, garden, farm, and fish. And together, they raised their children with spirituality, integrity, respect, understanding, and honor for Mother Earth and God the Almighty.

As a toddler Mazie could communicate with the horses far better than she could–or would–with humans. By age of five, Mazie would climb up a fence rail, leap onto her father's mare, and ride bareback with balance and ease. As she grew older, she continued to develop and perfected a uniquely affluent equine relationship. None in the valley had witnessed such a deep affinity with horses, let alone from a girl.

Mazie's only interaction with other people was with her younger brother Emiliano, and her native cousins. Her mother, Anna was an adept teacher, and Mazie, Emiliano, and several cousins were homeschooled with great success. Anna was known and admired for her heroic work to teach the native children to read and to survive in the white man's world. Both Mazie and Emiliano knew the basic conversation of their native language, but also learned fluent Spanish and proper English.

When Mazie was eight years old her mother was murdered. Anna was a half-mile from their home, up in the woods gathering pine nuts, when she came across three drunk white hunters. She tried to keep the situation under control, to peacefully tell the hunters that they were trespassing and needed to leave. One of the hunters knew who she was and began teasing her about wasting her time trying to teach the red—Indian heathens to read. The men's ignorance and drunkenness soon led from teasing to torment, and one of the hunters strangled her. All three men were charged with murder, but as was so deplorably common in those times, they were released three months later.

For his children, Ignacio pulled all the strength he could from God to overcome the loss of his Anna–and to overcome his hatred. Ignacio waited quietly in the depths of God's presence, striving to heal his thoughts amid God's holy whispers of Life... Peace... and Love. He experienced deep suffering, yet he could release his bitterness and live with an open heart despite it all. His forgiveness shined as a remarkable gift to the world.

Ignacio was not an educated man, barely able to read, yet he raised his children with a thirst for reading and knowledge. Mazie and Emiliano would take turns every night reading books to him. And it was customary for them to read from the Bible every night after supper. Both of his children honored and respected him. They knew that the best classroom in the world was by his side.

The first schoolhouse in Mimbres was built when Mazie was eleven. Mazie loved learning and had a thirst for knowledge but didn't enjoy being around the other children. Mazie was sent home the first week of school for wearing boys' britches. Dresses were to be worn to school by young ladies. Mazie didn't own a dress. She didn't tell her father why she was sent home. She simply went through the old wooden storage chest of her mother's things, found a skirt, put the skirt over her pants, tightened a belt around her waist to hold it in place, and wore it proudly the next day to school.

Mazie rode her mare to school bareback, with only a bridle to aid her in riding. Every day, she would ride up to school wearing her britches, when she arrived, she would unroll the skirt that she had tied in a bundle and stored on her back. Before entering the schoolhouse, she would wear the skirt over her pants and proudly enter the school.

Routinely, several of her horses would trail behind her on the way to school; they would forage freely while waiting for her to finish, then follow her home. The school children would make fun of her and her following of horses, thus earning her the nickname "Horse Girl" with the townspeople.

# Chapter 3

Outside the Santa Rita Mine office building, Mazie rode to the front of the building, sitting proudly on a magnificent Texas Quarter Horse. Rider and horse move skillfully yet gracefully toward Mr. Spenser Penrose and the large man adorned with a impressive display of medals on his military uniform. Mazie dismounted her horse in a simple, naturally elegant motion. With an emotionless expression, she spoke clearly in proper English. "Good morning, Mr. Spenser. I am returning your horse, Sir." Looking away from the two men toward the handsome horse, she petted his neck and smiled lovingly at the horse. "I have taught him a trick I think you will appreciate. Would you like to see what he can do for you?"

Penrose interrupted her display and grumbled gruffly, "Yes, of course, Miss Mazie. But first I would like to introduce you. This is Colonel Cambridge of the United State Army."

Mazie extended her hand. However, Colonel Cambridge refused her handshake and simply nodded his head.

Mazie immediately picked up on his negative energy. She thought, "This man has got to be the puffiest man I have ever seen." His body and face seemed swollen and grisly. She got chills, along with a sudden sickness in her stomach.

Penrose grunted, "Yes, yes, go on with your trick."

Mazie moved the horse back a few feet. She took a stick and pointed it to the ground in front of the horse's muzzle. The horse dropped his nose to the ground. Mazie took her stick and tapped his belly, followed by the tapping of his hocks on his hind legs. While he was buckling his hind legs, she tapped behind his front knees. He folded his front legs and gently laid down on the ground.

Many passing by townspeople, miners, and office workers watched in awe, and all ended with a bravo of clapping for Mazie's astonishing equestrian skill.

"Mr. Penrose, I know you have trouble mounting this tall steed, so I taught him to lay down for you so you can easily get on him." Her proud voice melted as she saw his expression convert to anger.

Penrose's face reddened with embarrassment. With macho pride, he screeched out, "Miss Mazie, I don't have trouble mounting my horse." Fumbling his words, he added, "Continue, what else did you train him to do?"

Mazie commanded the horse back on his feet and, with a swift, easy movement, dashed onto the bare back of the horse and commenced to show how tame and well-behaved the horse had become. With only a halter and without a saddle Mazie maneuvered the horse, and he responded to her every command.

Proudly, Mazie showed off the discipline, skill, and coordination of Penrose's steed. Just as she was finishing up her display, a Model—A horseless carriage drove up near them. When the car stopped, it shut down with a deafening bang. Neither horse nor rider was disrupted by the loud noise.

With his veins protruding from his forehead, Penrose labored from every step he took. He didn't like the attention Mazie was getting, and breathlessly he began to yell out orders, "You men, get back to work!" Gasping for air, he stammered, "Where is my son? Where is Junior?"

Colonel Cambridge licked his fat-purple lips and summoned Mazie. "Miss, do you mind stepping over here."

Mazie rode the horse over to him and dismounted. "Yes, Sir?"

"Young lady?" He asked, hoping to gather more information, "What is your surname?"

Abruptly, Penrose spat out the answer for her. "Miss Mazie's last name is Atencio." Even though she was recently married to his only son, Junior, he refused to acknowledge that her last name should now be Penrose. His blood pressure raged, and his stomach turned at the thought.

With self-importance, the Colonel continued, "Miss Atencio, as my friend Spenser introduced you before your beautiful display of equitation, I am Colonel Alexander Cambridge of the 34th Infantry Division of the United States Army. Perhaps you are familiar with our Regiment that is camped to the south of here near the town of Deming?" Prattling on without waiting for a reply from Mazie, he said, "As you might have heard, we have been commissioned by our Commander and Chief, President Woodrow Wilson. We are moving to the Western Front next week to help our allies in the ongoing war in Europe." Stating, "Or what some are calling The Great War." Conceit oozed from his every word. "The US Cavalry could use your talent in training the horses for our troops. Miss Atencio, the United States of America needs your help. Would you be interested in working with our cavalry? I am a powerful man with a very high rank in the US Army. I could easily have you commissioned."

Mazie swallowed hard and bravely kept her composure. "No thank you, Sir. My father has been very ill, and he needs me to care for him." Stunned by his proposal, it was all she could think of to say.

# Chapter 4

Heavenward, Mazie rode the western Mimbres high trail toward her favorite spot. Finding a place of peace, she stopped to look at the immense, glorious vistas around her. Mazie drew in a deep, cleansing breath. Then, with an all-embracing sweep, she looked to the west toward the Gila mountains with its towering conifer mountainsides and juniper-splattered foothills, and its life-vein, the Gila River meandering through the valley below. Around her, she viewed the prickly-pear cactus plants with petals the size of dinner plates, adorned with brightly colored blooms decorating the high-desert landscape. Tall, thick yucca trunks spiked up to the deep azure sky filled with billowing angelic clouds. Tranquility swept over her has she viewed her surroundings… It was Mother Nature's glorious canvas.

Mazie's horse bellowed softly, cooling and calming himself from the exertion of the climb. In an instant, both horse and rider were set on alert as a large rattlesnake with enormous rattles sounded out an alarm of his dangerous presence. Silently, without any spoken commands, Mazie skillfully, slowly, and gently backed her horse until she was ten feet away. Then she moved quickly, further back until she was twenty feet from the sounding, coiled-up snake. As there had been several sightings of mountain lions in this area, Mazie had her riffle loaded and ready by her side. With one precise shot, she hit the rattler, blowing off his head.

*   *   *

Mazie remembered a legend her mother's older brother had told her when she was a child. Rattlesnakes sometimes appear as divine punishment to strike vengeance on sinful people. Their Mimbres mythology told that the rattlesnake was the first creature to bring death into the world through its poison. This ancient wisdom of the feared and respected rattlesnake can be found etched in the petroglyphs in the Gila Cliff Dwellings.

Rattlesnakes tend to be viewed negatively in most Native American cultures frequently associated with violence and revenge. In the folklore of the Mimbres Tribe, the rattlesnakes were viewed as both powerful and dangerous. Children were taught that rattlesnakes were considered bewitching, and demanded respect for a rattlesnake bite is a punishment for wrongdoings.

Returning from her ride, as Mazie rode up to their house in Mimbres, she found a military horseless carriage parked outside. Slowly, she dismounted, walked up to the soldier stationed outside the door, and handed him the headless rattlesnake. "Here, hold this," Mazie said. The soldier's eyes widened, he briefly held onto the snake, then quickly threw it on a nearby stone. Mazie went in to find Colonel Cambridge sitting at the kitchen table with her papa and brother, Emiliano. Their conversation stopped upon her entering. Her brother's face was one of alarm, yet her papa was his usual calm and peaceful self as he greeted her calmly. "Ah, Mazie, my dear, Colonel Cambridge is here with a message from the US Army."

Emiliano quickly blurted. "You have been conscripted into the Army!" Then he handed her the draft notice.

Examining the document, she read it slowly in disbelief. It read:


SELECTIVE SERVICE NOTICE OF CONSCRIPTION

This document is a NOTICE OF CALL AND ORDER TO APPEAR FOR PHYSICAL EXAMINATION issued by the Local Board for the County of Grants, State of New Mexico. On this day, May 15th, 1917. Mazie Atencio is notified that she has been conscripted to serve for special duty by the United States. Mazie Atencio has been issued Serial No. 7490 with Order no. 425 and is to appear at the office of the In-Service Processing Office at Fort Cody, Deming, N.M. at 1:30 P. M. on May 17, 1917.

This notice is an official document issued by the Provost Marshall and Colonel Alexander Cambridge, Representative of the Local Board of the War Department.

* * *

The Colonel gave her ample time to read the legal scroll, then said authoritatively. "I have assured your father that you will not be involved in—or near any battles. You will receive a maximum salary of $28.05 per month as a Second Lieutenant." Continuing, "As I stated last week, the United States Army and our Allies need your extraordinary skills with our horses."

Mazie's face was stern as she voiced her stringent opposition. "No! You are mistaken. I will not go into the Cavalry." Stunned by the news, she paused briefly, then added proudly, "I must take care of my papa."

Expecting her reaction, her words did not affect Colonel Cambridge in the least. He informed her with taxing authority, "Miss Atencio, you have no choice in the matter. You have been drafted. You will be arrested if you do not report to the Service Processing Office at Fort Cody, Deming, by 1:30 P. M. on May 17th."

Proud of his generosity, he added in a by-the-way voice. "Also, I have arranged for your father to receive the medical treatment he needs at the Silver City Medical Center. I have arranged for a horse-drawn Army

Ambulance to pick him up tomorrow to transport him safely to the hospital."

Smugly, he said. "Miss Atencio, I will see you in two days in Deming, as stated in your summons. Good day." He stopped to shake hands with her father and brother, then turned around and left.

* * *

Mazie sank onto the kitchen chair, staring in disbelief into her papa's loving eyes. She was scrambling to understand what she had just been told. Fumbling for words, all she could say was, "I am not sure about this…" Shaking her head, "Any of this." "Papa?" She said, her emotions stirring and heaving as she searched for answers.

Calmly and reassuringly, her father Ignacio leaned over and placed her hands into his. "Mazie, my girl, remember all the books you have read to me over the years about other countries? This is your opportunity to see them firsthand. Dear girl, you are going to France. You can help our United States Cavalry doing what you love most by working with horses. And I'll be able to get the medical attention I need." He added, "Your brother will be here to take care of the ranch." His words were so full of love and hope. He was genuinely delighted for her. Bubbling with optimism, he added, "I am excited for you. I can't wait for you to return and tell us all about your experiences."

As if she had been holding her breath, Mazie let out a huge sigh. She had so many questions and concerns in her mind that she couldn't think of what to say. She tried to sound brighter than she felt, "But Papa, I've never been outside of Grant County. This is overwhelming. I am not afraid to go… But afraid of the unknown. And afraid of leaving you and Emiliano…"

Ignacio started coughing uncontrollably. Mazie and Emiliano had seen him suffer many coughing fits and waited patiently for him to stop. Ignacio's eyes sparkling with pride, he offered his inexhaustible wisdom to her. "Think of this opportunity as a lifetime experience. I am sure you are thinking to yourself that this is crazy. But you must remember that you are a loving, mighty warrior of God, hell-bent on changing the world. Be confident in yourself." Catching his breath, he added, "Be confident in God's goodwill." Kissing her cheek, he then said matter-of-factly. "And you are like the sun. Your heart and your presence brighten the world by sharing your light. You are like sunshine on a cool face. You have a beautiful energy and are capable of calm inner peace. Share your light. Share your peace."

Emiliano walked over to her and gave her a loving hug. "This is a great opportunity for you, Mazie. Papa and I will be fine here. I will take care of the ranch and check in on Papa at the hospital. Then I will bring him home when he is better."

Ignacio had not told them that he had been coughing up blood the past few days. He knew in his heart that he would not live long enough to see Mazie return from the war. He knew that Mazie could hold her own. She was a courageous woman with an unexplainable spark of life. It was rare for her to allow someone into her mystique. But when she did, you could see her magic. Mazie had clear awareness and radiated freedom. She belonged to nobody.

# Chapter 5

Emiliano loved and adored his sister and was apprehensive about Mazie being drafted into the cavalry. Yet, at the same time, he was envious that she would see parts of America in her travels to the coastal areas. And then traveling by boat to France.

Emiliano did not acquire his mother's semblance as his sister had. He was fair-skinned, with green-brown eyes and lighter hair and complexion than Mazie. He didn't share any of his sister's subdued mannerisms or her quiet demeanor. Emiliano was the master of persuasion, fiercely independent, and admired for his practical-minded thinking. He had a well-defined set of priorities and guidelines for life and often found solutions to logical problems much faster than others.

He was well-read and a self-taught archaeologist. Gila Cliff dwellings were only a three-hour horse ride, which allowed him to explore countless undiscovered sites. He was determined to unravel the history of the ancient

Mimbres and Mogollon people. Emiliano's reputation for being knowledgeable of the Gila area led him to employment as the lead scout for several historic expeditions. Scholars from the Smithsonian, Harvard, and Yale Universities, and many privately funded groups sought his services.

Reports of the first recorded Gila prospecting and archeology began around 1860, with private owners selfishly keeping or selling all the findings. Laws to protect and respect the prehistoric artifacts of the Gila dwelling and nearby sites didn't exist until the early 1900s.

With the help of Emiliano and the concerned citizens of the New Mexico Historical Society, thousands of pottery pieces and fully intact pots with beautifully detailed etchings and paintings were now recorded and preserved. They had found tools and axes of stone, finely crafted turquoise beads, sandals, baskets, corn cobs, arrowheads, prayer plumes, and prayer sticks. Their grand prize had been a rare find of four human mummies found at four different locations, all infants wrapped in cottonwood tree—fibers. All four mummies were recorded and sent to the Smithsonian. Appallingly, only one mummy ever made it there. Presumably, the other three had been stolen.

The US Forest Service finally stepped in to protect the Gila archeology sites, dwellings, and the hot spring house area through a proclamation in 1908. In 1912, the same year New Mexico became a state, the National Forest

Service established the Gila Cliff Dwellings as a National Monument.

* * *

A month earlier, Emiliano was invited to join a group of ranchers and archaeologists to discuss the Gila area. The conference was being held at the Palace Hotel in Silver City. Emiliano was scheduled to be a guest speaker. He spent hours preparing and practicing his presentation.

Dr. Forch of the US Army was the first to report to the group. "There are countless nearby ranches still hosting hundreds of untouched and unexcavated sites and dwellings, pictographs, and tributaries along the Mimbres River, the Black Range, and the banks of the West Fork of the Gila River." Clearing his throat and taking a sip of water, he continued to inform them. "Back in 1885, in the wake of an Apache raid that left thirty-five settlers dead, Lieutenant G. H. Sands and the troops of the 4th and 6th US Cavalry were sent to the Gila and Black Range area to protect and to keep the peace. The reports found from the young Lieutenant stated that he had read the sensationalized memoirs of Walter Prescott who wrote of diggings and findings of golden pots and golden utensils in the Gila cliff dwelling at the West Fork. Also, having read Prescott's history of the Incas and their treasures, Lieutenant Sands postulated that all ancient North American Indians had a surfeit of gold lying around. And he assumed that golden treasures would likely be discovered in the Gila Cliff Dwellings. Dishonorably,

Lieutenant Sands and his men reportedly ravaged and violated countless tributaries and artifacts in the area."

Emiliano thought to himself, "Gosh! He's a heavy-winded Buster," and he was grateful for him to end his lecture.

Emiliano spent much of his young life as a scout or an assistant archeologist for many privately funded prospectors. He loved the thrill of unearthing the remarkable history of his mother's people. He was proud of his heritage. It was as if he could feel their spirits and live their culture through his explorations. And he was equally proud that he was unearthing the history of the great Mimbres culture, descendants of the ancient Mogollon civilization which existed a thousand years before him. Their habitation in the areas was thought to date back from 10,000 BC, with recently found evidence showed human habitation from 500 BC.

William Knightly then read his report that the Mogollon ancestors who lived at the Gila Cliff Dwellings constructed and inhabited them between the late 1270s and 1300s. They were hunter-gatherers and farmers along the banks of the Gila River.

With great pride, Emiliano gave his narrative. "The Gila people left little writing, except for the symbolic petroglyphs on the rock walls. It has been speculated that a severe drought was probably the major factor in the civilization's departure, and the unstable climate led to widespread migration throughout Southeast Arizona, Northern Mexico, and Southwestern New Mexico. There is also evidence that a marauding enemy may have forced them to flee." Confidently, he continued. "Following the Mogollon people was the Mimbres tribe, who lived along the Mimbres River, the Gila River, and among the rugged Gila Mountains and Black Mountain Range. The Mimbres lived in compact pueblo-like villages of adobe and masonry, each village containing perhaps two hundred people. Because of sparse rainfall in the area, they relied on irrigation to grow corn—maize, beans, and squash; they also hunted small and large game. The Mimbres are perhaps most famous for their pottery, decorated with black-on-white designs of insects, animals, and birds or geometric lines." Clearing his throat he added, "I myself have many pots that have been passed down to me by my mother's Mimbres tribe. These pots tell a story about the folklore of their culture."

Emiliano continued, "The Apache entered this area shortly before 1600.

It is known that the Spanish interacted and coexisted peacefully with the native Mimbres people and the Apache during the 1600s and 1700s. By 1714, there were several Spanish settlements in this area, and in 1804, the Spanish established the Santa Rita Copper Mountain Mine settlement with a Spanish population of about eight hundred. In 1835, many Spanish settlers, including my grandparents, built a private fort at the mine, and many Spaniards established homesteads in the Mimbres Valley. Around 1820, American mountain men began trapping in the area. The Southwestern River Otter was prevalent and sought after by the trappers, and in a short time they have been over-trapped and shamefully are now extinct."

Emiliano went on to report, "Due to the upheavals caused by the Northern Apache, all Apache people, and the Mimbres people were forced onto a reservation that was set up near the Mimbres Valley in the 1850s. However, the discovery of gold in 1859 in Pinos Altos ended the agreement for the reservation, and the Native people were forced to move to San Lorenzo. The newly arriving Americans and Spaniards brought smallpox and disease, and in 1877, an epidemic annihilated many native cultures of New Mexico. In addition to the epidemic, a series of floods plagued the lands, causing the Apache and Mimbres people to settle throughout the Gila Mountain Range and the Black Range Mountains among the already dispersed Mimbres people throughout New Mexico."

Concluding his lecture, he said. "These proud nations blended and supported each other; eventually merging into one culture. Few could read or write, so much of their history and stories have been lost through time."

* * *

All in all, Emiliano felt the conference was a success. He had made many new contacts and was asked to join many upcoming seminars and excavations. Emiliano was excited to get home and tell his papa about it.

# Chapter 6

Mazie arrived at the Santa Rita Mine office at 8 a.m. per Colonel Cambridge's instructions. Standing out front was a young soldier in an army uniform. He wore knee- high boots wrapped in cloth, riding jodhpurs, a substantial belted jacket that buttoned up to just under his chin with military insignia on one arm and private designation on both. Rather than a helmet, he wore a leather cap with earmuffs and goggles hanging from a strap off the back.

"Excuse me," she asked the soldier. "I am supposed to get a ride to Deming, Camp Cody. Have they arrived yet?"

"That would be me, Miss," he said and pointed to a motorcycle with a sidecar.

Surprised by the means of her transportation, she said, "I am not riding for an hour in that strange mechanical contraption."

"Ahh, you must be the squaw they sent me to pick up. I'm told to deliver you for duty."

"You call me a squaw one more time, and I'll whup your lip wide open. And take that insulting sign off the side of your motorcycle."

"You mean this one?" Laughing, he pointed to the motorcycle's manufacturer logo, Indian.

"Yes." She said.

The soldier laughed and said, "Wait till I tell the Sarg! Hell! Girl, that is the name of the company that makes this motorcycle. Now, hop in the sidecar, or we'll be late, which means AWOL for you."

Mazie shoved her tote up in the nose of the sidecar and settled into the seat while the soldier handed her a pair of goggles.

"Better wear these, or your eyesight will be gone within the first mile." He informed her. They sped off for what Mazie was sure could be a long, bumpy, miserable ride.

Twenty miles into the ride, it suddenly occurred to her that she was enjoying the journey. She thought, "Well, this would be a half-day's ride on horseback, and sort of like riding horseback."

Later, they pulled off the main road where a sign hung. 'Cody Country Home of the 34th Infantry', The

Sandstorm Troopers. They then drove up to a building constructed with the bottom half wood and the top half a heavy tan-colored canvas. The driver got off the motorcycle, removed his goggles, and said abruptly, "Follow me." Entering the building, they found a gruff-looking man sitting behind a desk inside the front door.

"Private Dooley reporting with cargo as ordered, Sergeant."

"At ease". Barked the Sergeant.

"Young woman, I'm Sergeant Biggs. Do you have some paperwork for me?" Mazie handed him her paperwork.

Meanwhile, about ten feet away were some soldiers who were laughing and making Indian jokes. One scrawny Private said, "Yeah, that red skin squaw must be a really good whore to have been brought here to Fort Cody." He made it a point to talk loud enough for Mazie to hear. Mazie was used to the insults from the men at the Mine and in Silver City, but their joke hit a nerve. Mazie pretended to be amused by their jokes and approached them. She gestured with her hand in a 'come hither' wave until the Private was close enough for her to plant her riding boot to the lowest button on the fly on his government-issue britches. The soldier let out a scream and dropped to his knee instantly.

Sergeant Biggs leaped from behind his desk, grabbed Mazie, and barked a stern order for the men to back off. "Now you hold on there, Miss, you can't be hurting those men."

Returning to his desk, the Sergeant quickly typed up her orders and immediately sent Mazie to the nurse's station at the field hospital for a physical. After her quick exam, they handed her more paperwork to take back to Sergeant Biggs.

He briefly looked over the papers and said, "Congratulations, young lady, you have been deemed fit for service, to the Army of the United States of America!"

Continuing and raising his voice so the men nearby could hear him clearly, he said, "Raise your right hand." Sergeant Biggs swore Mazie in with just a few alterations from the regular Army jargon.

Surprised, he continued in a high-pitched tone, "Well, by golly! It says here in General Blocksom's orders, that you are to be instated into the U. S. Cavalry with the rank of Second Lieutenant." Sergeant Biggs looks over at the misbehaving brood that insulted her earlier. "Looks like you guys will be pressing the uniform and shining the boots of O-1 Atencio. Oh! And by the way, Lieutenant Atencio, you are out of uniform, so get yourself over to supply pronto and show them these orders, and they'll fix you up with the proper U.S. Cavalry uniform." He chuckled and offered a big grin. "So those boneheads can start saluting you."

He continued to bark orders, "Now, Lieutenant Atencio, you are to report back to the nurse's station at the hospital and they'll set you up with a bunk and locker in their billet." Laughing, he looked back over at the other men. "Who knows, you might even get a room to yourself, Lieutenant."

Sergeant Biggs knew that because of the sudden decision of the US's involvement in the Great War, the Army, Navy, and Marines recruited soldiers on the spot, and many recruits ranked fast.

* * *

The following day, Mazie reported back to the Sergeant. As she walked in, Sergeant Biggs stood at attention and saluted. Mazie just stood there with a weak smile.

"Lieutenant, you must return the salute." Said the Sergeant. "Well, I can see we need to indoctrinate you as to some simple military protocol before I take you over to meet the camp commander. Outside, they looked to find a place where the ground was level. He instructed her on saluting, when, how, and to whom to salute. And he taught her the correct posture for attention and parade rest.

Learning the command "At ease" was a given. However, following marching orders and being expected to obey them without reservation felt a little strange. Mazie was used to giving movement orders to a horse. It seemed ironic that the military boot, or horseshoe, was now on the other foot. Mazie quickly realized that she had been giving almost the same orders to horses her whole life.

The Sergeant usually expected problems with changing directions while marching, but Mazie surprised him with how effortlessly she executed her maneuvers. After finalizing her military commands, they took a five-minute walk to the camp command center. Sergeant Biggs suggested, "Just follow my lead, and everything will go just swell." They entered the General's office; the Sergeant promptly removed his hat and snapped to attention with an immediate salute. Mazie mimicked the Sergeant perfectly.

"At ease," said the General in a very relaxed fashion, even raised from his chair and smiled at Mazie. He started to seat himself, and he said, "Please have a seat." Continuing, "Lieutenant Atencio, when did you arrive at Fort Cody?"

The Sergeant started to blurt out, "Only about…"

"At ease Sergeant Biggs, I was addressing Lieutenant Atencio."

"I arrived here from Santa Rita yesterday, Sir".

"Lieutenant Atencio, I have been informed of your remarkable horsemanship and equestrian skill. The U.S. Army welcomes you and looks forward to you assisting our U.S. Cavalry. How long have you been working with horses?"

"Since I was a child, Sir."

"Extraordinary indeed!" The General cleared his throat and added, "Once again, I welcome you, Lieutenant Atencio into the service of The United States of America. And may God bless you!" A wee bit of prejudice came out in his next question. "You are a Christian I hope?"

Proudly she answered, "Yes, Sir, I believe Jesus Christ to be my Savior, General Sir."

"Splendid, glad to hear it, May God watch over you. I see you've been raised well and with respect. You may address me as either Sir or General Blocksom. As a lifelong horseman and proud member of the United States Cavalry, I want you to know how much I appreciate the skills with which you provide your country." The General stood, as did the Sergeant, and Mazie exchanged salutes. "Carry on. Dismissed, Lieutenant. Sergeant, dismissed"

Mazie caught a wink from the General as she performed a perfect about-face and left the office.

* * *

Mazie was released to return to her billet at the nurse's residence. A little later that day, an aide to Sergeant Biggs came knocking to inform Mazie that she was to report to Sergeant Biggs ASAP. Upon entering the Sergeant's office, Sergeant Biggs stood to attention and saluted her, then said with a big smile, "Lieutenant Atencio, it appears you will not be staying with us for long here at Camp Cody. At 06 hundred a week from today, you are to report back here for departure to El Paso, Texas. There you will board a train to Fort Sam Houston in San Antonio, Texas, where you will be attached to an AEFAG, also known as the American Expeditionary Force Advisory Group. You'll be assigned to the 2$^{nd}$ Cavalry Regiment under the command of General John Pershing." Without skipping a beat, he continued, "There, you will report to in-processing, where they will direct you to your reporting officer for quarters and your duty station. Good luck." Ending his orders, he saluted Mazie and she returned the salute.

* * *

After a week at Camp Cody, Mazie was driven in an Army vehicle to the El Paso train station with orders and a train ticket. The El Paso train station was an absolute rabble of chaotic ear-splitting noise and commotion. Mazie boarded and sat on the crowded civilian steam-engine train with several other troops. The train's whistle screamed, and off they went before several people were seated.

Mazie was exhausted and overwhelmed from a long intense day of training at Camp Cody, which had her quickly learn the commands, the does-and-don'ts, the who's-who, what-and-what's not, where-and-when…

After she was settled in, she proceeded to write her father a letter to let him know of her orders and whereabouts. She also started to write a letter to her husband Junior, but decided it would be a waste of time. She was reminded of her father's words. "A mistake that makes you humble is better than an achievement that makes you arrogant."

Usually, Mazie was silent and wanted to avoid chatting with people. However, she befriended the sweet couple sitting in the seat in front of her. The bubbly young woman boasted about how they were on their honeymoon. Mazie enjoyed talking with them, yet she was grateful that they got off the train in Pecos, Texas, for they had been a constant reminder of her ridiculous marriage to Junior.

She took a trip to the attic of her memory. Spenser Penrose Jr. was a small man lacking the balls to stand up to any man, let alone his father. He was a sissified man of all talk and glorified stories. Mazie first met Junior when he had commissioned her and her brother Emiliano to be guides on a short hunting trip in the Gila Mountains. Junior quickly became infatuated with Mazie. After the hunting trip, he created several jobs training horses at his father's Mine so he could spend more time with her. Junior wooed her, sent her notes of love, and showered her with cheap gifts.

After a month of courting, Junior took advantage of his father being away on business. He picked up Mazie in his new shiny, horseless carriage. Junior took her for her first ride in an automobile to Silver City. He wined, dined, and romanced her with his fake cowboy grandeur. Mazie had never drunk alcohol nor received any romantic attention from a man, and she impetuously fell for his charm. Junior had arranged for a drunkard Silver City Municipal Judge Vincent Horn to perform their nuptials, and compulsively, Mazie agreed to marry him.

After the ceremony, Junior drove Mazie back home to tell her papa the news, and away they went to the Santa Rita Hotel for their honeymoon. Junior continually dominated every conversation. And sex with Junior was so one-sided it seemed that Mazie was only posing as an object to fuck. Never were her needs or her pleasures considered or asked about.

It didn't take her long to realize her enormous marital mistake, and she used her father's illness as a need for her to stay at home and care for him. It than became a regular excuse, so she would not have to spend time with Junior. Mazie's father went along with her wanting to stay home with him.

When Junior's father, Spenser Senior, learned of their marriage, he became so enraged with his bone-headed sons' atrocious elopement that he sent Junior away on business to Bisbee, Arizona, for several months. Mazie had not seen or heard from him since.

# Chapter 7

The next scheduled train stop would be Fort Sam Houston, Mazie's new duty assignment in San Antonio, Texas. Mazie was grateful for disembarking the train and immediately checked in with her reporting officer, then promptly went to the fort's stables. She visited with the horses and met several men with whom she would continue on with her deployment to Hoboken, New Jersy. Still needing to walk about, she wandered into one of many mess tents including, a large kitchen set up to feed the troops.

Mazie noticed a petite woman of Spanish descent and greeted the young women in the kitchen. She spoke to her in Spanish. "Buenos dias Señora, what a wonderful kitchen you have here."

The young woman beamed with pride and said with a childlike voice in Spanish. "Thank you." Wiping her hands on her flour-sack apron, she extended her hand to Mazie, and they shook hands.

"It must be hard work to feed all the troops?" Mazie questioned.

"Si, verdadero, it is," she gushed, so excited to talk to her in her native language. "Mi querida, it is nice to be in the presence of another woman." Giggling through her words, she added, "There is nothing but stinky boys around here." She snarled her nose.

Mazie released a short laugh and a smile, something she rarely offered. She added gratuitously, "I look forward to your comida."

She had an instant bond with the cook. Aurelia Huerta was from the nearby town of Laredo. It was a treat for Mazie to be able to speak Spanish with someone, and the two immediately took a liking to each other. The two spent several hours talking about their families, and hometowns, and compared stories about the slayings and massacres of the legendary revolutionist Pancho Villa and his gang.

Mazie told Aurelia that earlier last year, Pancho Villa and his men had gunned down thirty men, women, and children in the nearby border town of Columbus, New Mexico, and wounded dozens of others. It was a little too close to home, Columbus was only a half-day ride from her home in Mimbres.

In March 1916, Villa planned a raid on the military garrison in the small town of Columbus, New Mexico. Villa sent spies to gather information, and they returned to report that the garrison consisted of only fifty men. On a dark night in March, Villa led his army into Columbus and attacked the garrison. Villa's men also began looting and setting fire to houses in the town. However, rather than the fifty U.S. soldiers that Villa's scouts had previously reported, there were three hundred and fifty soldiers, which included the 13th U.S. Cavalry from nearby Camp Cody in Deming. Villa's Army suffered many losses, yet the filthy bastard rode back into Mexico only to ravage, rape, and murder more innocent people.

Tears filled Aurelia's eyes as she somberly informed Mazie, "Both my Madre and Padre and my Tio were killed by Pancho Villa and his men when they stormed my hometown." Wiping the tears from her eyes, "I was working at a nearby ranch and escaped any harm."

Aurelia paused to reflect, then continued. "Captain Patton brought me here to Fort Houston to cook for him and his men. I am really enjoying it here. "Her eyes suddenly filled with delight, "Mi querida, I even met a wonderful man here."

Her sadness was quickly replaced with a face beaming with joy as she told Mazie, "His name is Miguel." Laughing, she corrected herself, "I mean Michael, Michael Sullivan." Giggling, she then whispered, "He is a white man, so I've got to get used to calling him that."

* * *

Every day at the Fort, the men would watch Mazie work with the horses. She rapidly gained the attention and respect of many of the troops. Numerous men asked if they could join her in the training corral, listened, and studied her training techniques.

A week after she arrived at the Fort, Mazie received a personally written invitation from Captain George Patton to join him and his friends at the Grande Nobel Hotel in San Antonio. For hours after receiving the invitation, she nervously pondered on how to turn it down. But the last thing Mazie needed was to get caught in a lie with such a well-known and respected officer of the United States Army. She borrowed one of the Cavalry horses and rode into town to the library to find a book on the proper etiquette and table manners at a formal dinner party. She checked out the book "A Ladies Book of Etiquette", by Jean Clark, and that night Mazie and Aurelia read the book. Mazie nervously practiced, and Aurelia laughed and teased her.

Some of her new friends from her battalion offered to drive her to the dinner, but she decided to travel by horseback. Her thought was that she would be much calmer if she did so. On the day of the dinner, she picked out her favorite horse from the corral. She washed and groomed him, and she drew his fearless, tranquil, and gentle energy to help her with her confidence and composure. The horse appeared to be of wild Mustang heritage. He was light-tan all over, except for dark tones on his forelegs and muzzle, which gave the steed a concentrated, pointed look of strength and native nobility.

Aurelia helped Mazie to get ready by cleaning and pressing Mazie's uniform. Aurelia brushed and neatly braided Mazie's long black hair.

Mazie decided she would be more comfortable riding the steed bare-back. And she rode the noble mustang with confidence, poise, and pride as she made her way to the hotel.

When she entered the plush dining room of the opulent Grande Nobel Hotel, Captain Patton and all but one man stood. And the three women who were seated at his table just stared at her.

"Lieutenant Atencio, welcome." He then introduced the other two men and three women seated at the table.

Keeping a stalwart composure, she greeted the other guests. "Good evening." She stood with pride in her culture and equanimity. The women, who were dressed to the nines, never acknowledged her or made any eye contact with her. Mazie had never seen such beautiful dresses and apparel and wanted to ask them about their dresses, but never got up the nerve.

One of the other officers present, Lieutenant Franklin, promptly began boasting about Mazie. "Lieutenant Atencio, I have witnessed your remarkable work with taming and training our Cavalry horses, and I want to thank you for your service."

Mazie replied, "Thank You, Sir."

Captain Patton seemed genuinely sincere and chimed in, "Yes, Lieutenant Atencio, your reputation precedes you. Many of the men kept boasting about the new Lieutenant who works wonders with horses. So, I had to go see for myself earlier in the week. Lieutenant, you have quickly become a legend." Adding, "The response you get back from the horse to your every command is remarkable. I have never seen anything like it".

"Thank you, Captain Patton." She said with a proud spirit.

The man sitting directly across from her at the table was introduced to her as Louis Miller from Lexington Kentucky. She found him continually staring at her. Ludicrously he announced with all of his snobberies in a thick southern drawl, "I have heard that the red skin Indians are exceptional in their horsemanship. Nonetheless, you must admit, Captain Patton, that having a woman in the Army is appalling, and the Army is asking for trouble".

Captain Patton dismissed Louis' rude remark and immediately changed the conversation to his tales of Pancho Villa and his bandits, how Pancho Villa eluded him and was still on the run.

The woman sitting next to Captain Patton leaned nearer to him and placed her gloved hand on his arm. She purred like a kitten in a creamery, "Captain Patton, you are so brave to pursue that horrible villain."

Mazie kept mentally referring back to the proper table instructions she read in the book of etiquette, and was grateful that she had taken the time to read the book. She stopped to examine the silverware set at the table and decided which of the many utensils she should be using. She did take two sips of wine out of politeness. Remembering the first and last time she drank wine, she ended up marrying Junior.

After dinner, Mazie politely offered her thanks and bid farewell. On her ride back to the camp, she replayed the evening. She was strong and proud of herself and grateful for the opportunity to have learned so much from this experience. Mazie had never before encountered society people in her lifetime. It certainly had not been her first experience with men of bigotry and racism. Her father taught her long ago that when people are rude, harsh, critical, or argumentative, she needs to recognize that it is not really about her. And that she needs to remain tenacious and resist the urge to react. She smiled as she heard her father's words in her head. "Do not allow their ignorant behavior to steal your pure energy or steal your peace".

* * *

After Mazie had left the dinner party, Louis Miller told the group the heroic story of Captain Patton's chase for Pancho Villa. He told them it had been a year earlier in May 1916, that General John Pershing and Second Lieutenant George Patton had led an American military expedition into Mexico in search for the elusive Villa and his men, known as "Villistas".

* * *

General Pershing was romantically involved with Second Lieutenant Patton's sister, Nita, at the time, and the General offered the young officer the opportunity to participate in the expedition as his aide.

Riding in three Dodge horseless carriages, General Pershing ordered Second Lieutenant Patton to lead a detachment of seven soldiers and two interpreters to a nearby farm, where they might buy provisions and gain information from the locals. General Patton then pushed on to the small town of Las Cienega. At the farm, the Lieutenant questioned Villas' lead Lieutenant Cardenas' uncle, and without gaining much information, they followed a small lead to San Miguelito. When the soldiers noticed someone running inside when they neared the San Miguelito ranch house. Alarmed, Patton ordered six men to cover the house, while two more swept along a wall to the south. Armed with a rifle and pistol, Patton moved quickly beside a wall to the north. Suddenly, three men on horseback burst from the building and charged toward the soldiers. Their way blocked, they turned and came straight at Patton, who open-fired and shattered one rider's left arm, who then crawled out of sight.

Another rider came at Patton, who fired again. Both horse and rider tumbled. When the remaining band of la guerrillas stood and drew their weapons, Patton and the other soldiers gunned them down. Just then, a third rider who was intent on escaping managed to get a hundred yards out, was spotted by several soldiers who opened fire, and he fell to the ground. Later, he was identified as Cardenas. The soldiers shot him again, and as he lay on the ground, more soldiers approached. Cardenas feigned surrender, yet he reached for his gun. In a flash, he was shot in the head.

No one at the scene would positively identify the dead men, and their bodies were tied to the hoods of the cars. As they quickly fled the area, they could see a group of at least forty hostile horsemen approaching, and Second Lieutenant Patton ordered a rapid retreat to Pershing's headquarters. An impromptu burial followed after someone positively identified Cardenas' body.

It was a burial, but indeed not a funeral. One soldier who looked on muttered, "Ashes to ashes, dust to dust…If Villa won't bury you, Uncle Sam must."

General Pershing was pleased with Second Lieutenant Patton and permitted him to keep Cardenas' sword and saddle. The incident made headlines across the United States, and Patton was hailed a hero. He loved the limelight. Destined for even greater fame, he received a quick promotion to First Lieutenant and was made captain within a year.

Three weeks quickly passed, and Aurelia and Mazie met every day after Aurelia had fed the troops. Mazie and

Aurelia admired the moonlight, talking and dreaming. Aurelia's face lit up one evening as she danced around, and said, "Mi querida, I am so happy! Michael has asked me to marry him." She beamed with love. "And I know he cannot afford a fancy wedding or wedding band…" Sighing, "But I am sad that I will not have the traditional wedding celebration that my parents would have given me, and they will not be here to enjoy my wedding day." Cheering up, she added, "But I have to be okay with that, I just want to be Michael's wife."

Mazie responded in a spur-of-the-moment tone, "Let me help you and Michael." Mazie removed her wedding ring, placed it in Aurelia's hand, and curled Aurelia's figures around the golden band. "Please take my ring, and you can use it for your wedding."

Aurelia teared up as her brow raised in wonder, "But Miss Mazie, I cannot…"

Determinedly Mazie stopped her, "Trust me, it will do you a lot more good than it does for me. Please, this is my gift to you and Michael."

# Chapter 8

With the intent of helping in the war effort, the United States government, by—law took over all trains, guaranteeing their return after the end of the war. Mazie's train ride to Hoboken was in a luxury car, which she wasn't too sure if she could be comfortable with, as she had never been in any vehicle, carriage, or home so fancy. She shared the car with three other Cavalry lieutenants. Mazie was never much for conversations; she would rather listen and learn. If the topic wasn't about horses, she rarely joined in the discussions.

Mazie was looking forward to seeing a lot of the country on the three-day ride which was scheduled to include brief stops in cities on the way to the New Jersey coast. She remained constantly busy with animal care, and meetings regarding the preparation for the train's arrival, unloading, and then reloading onto the transport ship.

She was truly enjoying herself and was delighted to see so much of the country on her train ride, glued to the window. Just inside the eastern border of Texas, the train passed through the Alabama-Coushatta Indian Reservation. As the train slowed to a crawl, Mazie became curious about what may have slowed down the train. Looking out her window she witnessed around forty or fifty indigenous people walking along the tracks, carrying heavy bundles on their backs. Some had small children on their hips. Travois—manually pulled sleds made of latilla poles and hide, carried their elderly. She could see their weathered faces filled with anguish, suffering, and pain. Mazie's soul cried with profound sadness for her native kinsmen and she felt shamed over their mistreatment by the United States Government.

Originally, the Alabamas and Coushattas tribes lived in adjacent areas of the Alabamas Territory. By 1780, the tribes had migrated to East Texas, where they settled in a region known as **Big Thicket** and adapted their culture to the environment of forests and waters. Although they were two separate tribes, the Alabamas and Coushattas had stayed closely associated throughout their history.

Under aggressive pressure from European American settlers, the Alabamas and Coushattas were continually being pushed off their land. Unlike many Native Americans, they had received protection in the late 18th century under Spanish rule. The Texas area continued to be settled, yet the tribes established friendly relations and traded with the new homesteaders. And, again, unlike most Native American tribes, Sam Houston helped protect them during years of conflicts with other Native Americans in the area. After the annexation of Texas by the United

States, settlement increased, and the tribes' people were under pressure again as settlers began to take over their land. Triumphantly, they appealed to the state of Texas to have land set aside for their exclusive use. However, they lived in the extreme property.

Mazie could remember her uncle telling her and her brother Emiliano stories about the horrific treatment of its Indigenous people as the "Original Sin" of the leaders throughout the history of the United States. It has become the systematic destruction of the Native peoples of North America. The White supremacy of the United States was built on a foundation of colonization, racism, and genocide.

The Native American's inherent sanctity is filled with rich traditions of faith and spirituality. Before colonizers landed on this continent, Native Americans organized themselves into tribal nations and powerful confederacies. The White reaction to the cultural and political power of Native Americans has been genocide legitimized by the creation of legal authority and institutional control, and this ghastly system of White supremacy still flourishes in the United States.

From the first interactions with Native Americans, the White men were fueled with the destruction of Native Americans in North America as they have worked toward one thing, and that is theft. The theft of their land, theft of their natural resources, theft of culture and identity.

Throughout history, White supremacy has demonstrated its power to reshape institutions and supersede justice. President Andrew Jackson signed the Indian Removal Act of 1830, ordering the removal of all

Native Americans from their tribal land and then forcing them to live on reservations. The Supreme Court initially attempted to side with the tribes, who had signed treaties that ensured their national sovereignty. However, President Jackson bypassed the courts and bent the strength of federal institutions to further meet the needs of white supremacy. President Jackson oversaw the forced relocation of a hundred thousand Native Americans at the hands of national and local military forces, resulting in the loss of ancestral homelands and fifteen thousand deaths from exposure, disease, and starvation.

On December 26, 1862, six days before signing the Emancipation Proclamation, President Abraham Lincoln ordered the hanging of thirty-eight Dakota men, which was the largest mass execution in U.S. history. These men had taken part in a Native uprising in response to broken treaties. This shows us the racist legal system created to suppress, control, and remove Native Americans. The United States made countless treaties promising to end the stealing of Native lands. Then, the US quickly allowed the treaties to be annulled and violated. In addition, the White men made Native Americans' resistance punishable. Thus, they continued pushing Native Americans out of their homes, off of their lands, and into smaller areas of land. White settlers desired gold, timber, buffalo and land, and used this abhorrent legal system and institutions to steal it all from the tribes many of whom depended on their land's resources for their survival.

Boarding schools for Native children, often run by Christian organizations, were created to desecrate Native identities. At one such school, the motto was "Kill the Indian, Save the Man." Native children were required to cut their hair, wear uniforms, speak only English, and take anglicized names. Children could legally be kidnapped from their families by the U.S. government and forced to attend these boarding schools. During much of our nation's history, the federal government outlawed Native American religious practices. When Native Americans refused to have their culture stolen from them, the federal government responded with violence, exemplified by the needless slaughter as witnessed in the Wounded Knee Massacre in 1890, which was only 27 years earlier.

Mazie said a silent prayer for all the Indigenous people. "Dear God, through your unending love, bring us all into a Circle of Oneness. In this circle, may we learn to respect, honor, and celebrate our diversity and our differences as one human family. I pray that our government leaders will be filled with your wisdom and your peace. And I pray that our government respects native people and their lands."

* * *

A few days into her travel, Mazie found a used Dime Novel that had fallen under her seat and decided to read it. It was "The Two Scouts" written by Edward S. Ellis in 1877. She had heard much scuttlebutt about the popular Dime Novels, and her curiosity got the best of her, she decided to read it. It was both amusing and insulting to see how Native Americans were portrayed in the novel. However, it did give her a glimpse of understanding of how Americans thought of her people and how their ignorance and callousness may cause some people to be afraid. Becoming tired of sitting in her cabin, she decided to visit the horses, where she climbed up onto a large white gelding, and read the novel to the horses contained in one of the five cattle cars.

* * *

1860, the first dime novels were published around the start of the American Civil War. These sensational stories were full of romance and adventure and became wildly popular in both the United States, England, and English-speaking European countries, where they were known as "penny dreadfuls." Named for their low prices, dime novels were distributed in numerical series at newsstands and dry goods stores for a dime or a nickel a piece. No mind games or head trips, only simple storytelling. The first of these stories was about the American Indians, but when Indians were forced onto reservations, the public's fascination with them began to fade. Consequently, the novels morphed into stories of cowboys in the Wild West, outlaws and bandits, and train robbers. Dime novels typically tell the dramatic adventure stories of a single hero or heroine who often found himself or herself amid a moral dilemma. The novels were ethically sound, endorsing good character and strong moral values when the novel's hero chose virtue over vice. Sometimes, the protagonist was a historical figure, sparking the young readers' interest in history. From the battles with the Indians and the events of the Civil War, readers were looking for high-action stories about the West.


* * *


As her journey continued eastward, Mazie managed to get glimpses of the South as the train traveled to New Orleans, and Mobile, Alabama, before heading north toward Atlanta, Georgia. After yet another stop to fill up with coal and water, the train kept moving along the eastern slopes of the beautiful Appalachian Mountain Range in Georgia and then through South and North Carolinas, passing through Virginia, and then a grand view as the train passed through the middle of the nation's capital, Washington D.C. The train continued northward through Baltimore, and Philadelphia and headed to the port of Hoboken, New Jersey. Mazie utilized this downtime to meditate and pray. Mazie loved seeing God's artistry as she traveled through the States. She loved seeing so much greenery. On several occasions, she took in deep breaths as if she could inhale the green. She sent gratitude to God as she discovered this beautiful world. The magnificence of existence was breathtakingly and overwhelmingly beautiful. The stunning grace of God was all around her. Mazie recited a Psalms verse from the Bible, "Out of Zion, the perfection of beauty, God shines forth."

# Chapter 9

First settled by Europeans in 1643, the Hoboken Port of Embarkation was located in the city of Hoboken, on the waterfront in Hudson County of New Jersey.

The designation as a port of embarkation meant national fame for Hoboken. When soldiers left the city's ports, General John J. Pershing promised the troops they'd be in "Heaven, Hell or Hoboken" by Christmas of 1917, and it became a national rallying cry for a swift end to the war. Millions of American servicemen passed through Hoboken on their way to and from Europe. Congress had recently passed the Selective Service Act, requiring American men ages twenty-one to thirty to register for the draft, and millions of had registered. Hoboken was once primarily a German community in New Jersey, with nearly 25 percent of its 70,000 residents either German-born or the children of German immigrants. All German-born residents because of their German heritage were required to register as "enemy aliens," and hundreds lost their jobs, homes, and businesses.

* * *

As Mazie's train reached the Port of Hoboken, it had to enter the port at a crawling pace to avoid the American protesters blocking passage into the dock.  Gratefully, most of the protestors were more concerned about hindering the ships that were loading US troops of the American Expeditionary Forces. They were currently loading onto the naval ship the Covington II, loading up the 3,385 men and women headed to Saint Nazaire, where it was reported they would be greeted and helped by the thousands of volunteer French locals to help get them to Paris.

Mazie and several soldiers who had been assigned to help with the horses immediately got busy unloading the 96 horses that came off the crated train cars. they were transferred to the make-shift corral that was supposed to hold the horses before loading them on the S.S. Quinault, destined to France. The corral containment area was a gross, muddy mess from the recent rains and the hundreds of horses being moved. Mazie was having a hard time throwing their grass hay on the muddy ground to feed the horses in fear that they might digest some of the mud and cause colic. She did manage to ensure that the horses were given fresh clean water. She spent most of the afternoon and into the late evening caressing, cooing, and petting them trying to reassure them they would be all right and to help keep them calm. Knowing that horses would easily pick up on her anxiousness, she strived to keep herself calm and peaceful. This was easy for her because being around so many horses was her spiritual elixir.

As far as she could see, horses were in both directions along the dock. Seeing so many horses was a dream come true, yet it made her sick to think what these noble steeds were about to face once they got to France. There were mules, donkeys, draft horses, big horses of all kinds and colors, and small horses of every size and color.

One of the horses from the train she had been on, she had become fond of. It was a large white gelding, about 16 hands tall, and because of his size, she called him Hercules. Oddly enough, there were not a lot of white horses in New Mexico, so her heart was taken by him. He was a beast of a gentle giant and responded well to her every command. She continually reminded herself not to get attached to any of the horses, but her heart blended with Hercules. At dusk, Hercules was still antsy and having trouble adjusting to the hundreds of horses around him. Mazie climbed up on his back and laid quietly on top of him.

Mazie heard a commotion among the horses in the nearby corral and caught sight of a small man wearing all black moving in and around the horses. She watched as he dumped buckets of liquid into their water troughs and then she noticed he had a syringe and was injecting them with something. She realized that he was up to no good. Quietly, she slipped off the back of Hercules. She ducked down among the horses, trying not to be seen, quietly crawled under and around the horses, and finally made her way to the far end of the dock, to the office that housed the Military Police.

She woke up an MP sleeping in his chair. "Sergeant, come quickly. A strange man with a syringe moves within the horses and is injecting them with something."

Startled, the Sergeant kicked the feet of three other MPs, "Wake up! And come quickly."

Catching her breath, she shouted at the MPs "There is a strange man harming the horses."

Mazie and the four MPs raced to where she had seen the suspicious man.

"There he is, there," Mazie pointed him out.

The natural wildcat in Mazie emerged and with all her bravado she outran the others and body-slammed the man, who went flying to the ground. The man quickly jumped up and punched Mazie in the chin. Instantly, several MPs then tackled the intruding culprit to the ground. A passing Cavalry officer noticed the scuffle, pulled his side arm, and fired a warning shot into the air, stopping any more commotion.

The sergeant was instantly concerned for Mazie. She reassured him, "I am okay, please don't worry." Pointing her finger at the villain. "Just take care of him." The Sergeant wet his handkerchief in a nearby water trough and pressed on Mazie's chin.

All the commotion had brought two dozen more soldiers to the scene.

Mazie followed the MPs and the apprehended man to the MP's office. The man was carrying a briefcase, a paper bag containing glass vials, and glass syringes filled with a thick slimy yellow liquid.

* * *

After much investigation, it wasn't until the S.S. Quinault was out to sea that they discovered further information. They discovered that the man was a German spy.

The yellow liquid, which carried fatal bacteria, had been cooked up in what was known as "Tony's Lab," by an American-born German espionage agent named Dr. Anton Dilger.

German espionage and sabotage in the United States had been going on long before the United States formally entered the war in April 1917. Dilger's work was just one of many ways the Germans sought to undermine America's ability to aid its allies. Fewer horses and mules would make moving artillery and other war materiel much more difficult; it had become a strategic priority for Germany.

Anton's grandfather had also been a German medical doctor, so, unsurprisingly, Anton was sent at the age of nine, to study medicine in Germany. Dilger passed the medical exam at the University of Heidelberg in 1908 and by 1909 was an assistant at the university surgical clinic while researching his doctoral dissertation. While studying microbiology and germ culture, he learned how to set up a medical culture lab. Ironically, his research was on how to prevent the vicious bacterial infections, killers of horses, mules, and other animals.

When the War began in 1914, all German-born residents of the US were required to register as "Enemy Aliens". It is surprising and disappointing that many espionage agents such as Dilger disappeared into American society and committed so many cowardly and criminal acts.

# Chapter  10

One of the many responsibilities of the port's dockyard and embarkation facilities at Hoboken New Jersey, was to facilitate freight transfer onto the ship. Equipment was not an issue. However, loading the horses was a different matter. The live equestrian freight had been held in the train's open-air cars, which had to first be emptied of the horses. Then, they were led into massive wooden corrals, and temporary rope-made holding areas. This was followed by the laborious task of hoisting the precious cargo one by one onto the enormous 439-foot- long S.S. Quinault. Every horse was placed into a heavy rope, canvas-made sling, or a loading box. Each horse being lifted one-by-one using giant cranes onto the landing on the ships deck.

Once each horse was on board, they were donned with protective gear consisting of head bumpers, leg wraps, and shipping blankets. Each equine commando was immediately escorted into a narrow, independent stall where they would endure the 12 to 15-day-long journey across the Atlantic Ocean. The dock men labored to load horse hay, meals, and provisions for the people on the ship, along with enough water for both man and beast.

While the shore crew was busy transferring the horses from the equestrian train cars to the ship, many of the cavalry soldiers spent time with their horses, allowing both horse and rider to decompress from their train ride. This transfer took all day and into the night before military personnel boarded and the ships pulled away from the dock for their 3,468-mile voyage.

Mazie shared her ship's quarters with nine American nurses headed to the military camps in Paris and Chateau-Therry. Mazie had never been in the company of many women, and at first, she found their endless chatter and twitter very annoying, so she kept to herself, utilizing her spare time to meditate and pray. She rarely joined in their conversations, politely speaking only when asked a question.

In the middle of the second night at sea, a Cavalry soldier franticly summoned Mazie up on deck to the horse stalls. Upon arriving on the deck of the ship, she saw the horror of several of the horses who had collapsed and were unconscious in their stalls. Her heart sank as she franticly rushed to the horses quickly triaging the situation. There were several men there anxiously viewing the conditions of the fallen horses. Mazie could hear the spirits of the horses crying in anguish. She said a quick prayer before continuing to check on the other horses, the tension ebbing as they inspected every stall for more dead horses. Men were shouting at each other as they discovered another dead horse. The investigation confirmed that eighteen horses were dead.

The veterinarian on board, Edward Sylvester, and the ship's Commander, Charles Mawson, came onto the horrific scene. Flustered and stunned, Mazie informed them of the man that they had apprehended back at the dock at Hoboken.

The men worked well into the night, dragging the dead animals out of their diminutive stalls and using the ship's crane to hoist the horses overboard into the omnipotent sea.

After the last horse was dumped overboard, Mazie said a silent prayer to the sea. She summoned the creatures of the sea to be blessed with spiritual sustenance from the horses who had passed on and were now offered their nourishment. Trembling, Mazie sank to her knees and screamed a writhing cry of agony and rage. Then again, she said a silent prayer, this time up to the heavens. The warrior in her would not release any tears, yet her soul was eviscerated with anguish and pain.

Mazie sat on the ship's deck for several hours and looked out over the moonlit water. She was in awe over the power and the vastness of the mighty sea. She sat and witnessed the changing colors of the sky at dawn onto the ocean. She was totally awe-struck by the immensity of the endless sky and water. Breathing in the fresh air and finding peaceful nourishment, she returned to her chambers. The echoes of the horses' crying spirits rang in her mind. One of the sweet nurses named Adeline came over to offer comfort. She said with a voice as peaceful as a lullaby, "I am truly sorry for the loss of the horses, and that you had to bear witness to their devastation." Tearing up, she added, "Somewhere in heaven's own space, they are there in blissful sweet pastures with the accompaniment of a delightful singing creek. It will be their own paradise." Adeline gave Mazie a gentle, caring hug.

Adeline's words were of little comfort, yet the hug she shared with Mazie was beautiful, meaningful and mending.

In the days following, Mazie kept herself busy up on deck, visiting with the horses, brushing them, and petting them. She got to know several of her fellow Cavalrymen. She enjoyed learning where they were from. All the men from the northern states and east coast treated her with respect. Yet many of the men from the south, southwestern states, and California held prejudiced minds and hearts toward her and the First Nations People.

She spent her evening meals in the mess hall with her new friend, Adeline Jones. They enjoyed each other's company and Adeline even got Mazie to laugh out loud a few times. Mazie's laughter was a gift she rarely permitted.

# Chapter 11

Their original port of entry was planned to be the Port of Brest, France, however, they were diverted south to Saint-Nazaire because of recent activity by German U- boats that sank any and all ships through the English Channel.

The enormity and capabilities of Port Saint-Nazaire were almost too much to take in for any rank of soldier. The Harbormaster was busy preparing the twelve outgoing railroad track lines, alerting the French Army regarding new arrivals, and arranging for the ships to dock next to the adjoining railroad tracks.

General Pershing was already in France waiting at the docks to meet the US Cavalry. His strategic deployment, unit details, and special disembarking considerations were absolutely essential. The 2$^{nd}$ Cav would be going in four separate destinations: The 2nd and 3$^{rd}$ squadrons would be headed south to Pauillac to set up operational headquarters of the US Cavalry; M troop would head straight east close to the Swiss border to section off a significant push by the German Army out of Switzerland. Just to the north, F and G troops would be assisting the French as they pushed the German Army fifty miles back to the German border. Mazie would be with Troops A and C as they joined allies at a major campaign in Saint Germain near the Marne River. The region of the Marne River had previously been made legendary for the most horrific battles in the history of warfare.

General Pershing was a doyen of logistics. The imported railcars were American Baldwin engines and cars sent over to replace the remaining war-damaged French trains. So began transferring cargo, horses, and troops onto cars. It would be executed in reverse loading from the Port in Hoboken. It took all of two days to send off the first wave, free up the railroad tracks for the second wave, and so on for the third and fourth waves. So intently focused on Mazie's duties, she didn't notice much of the other activity stopping on the docks. Many French dock hands could not take their eyes off the striking exotic woman, who was outworking the men around her.

Lack of sleep from the voyage and the task of overseeing the handling and care of the horses, donkeys, and mules onto the train cargo cars had Mazie exhausted and near collapse. The ship's disembarkation continued in waves, with everything transferred onto railroad cars. With absolutely no rest for the weary, Mazie labored late into the night, until she finally took the opportunity to quickly eat some rations and then managed to get a little sleep in one of the cargo cars where her new equine friend Hercules was kept.

The next morning, Mazie awoke to a startling, scary moment. She had been so tired she didn't remember falling asleep. Mazie could tell she hadn't moved because the blanket was still across her just as she draped it over herself on her makeshift bed. She had no idea where she was for the first fifteen or twenty seconds, until she saw the white gelding Hercules standing nearby. The commotion in the harbor was coming alive and resuming its almost ear-shattering machinery noise, and men yelling out to each other.

Not much preparation was needed to resume her tasks as she had fallen asleep fully dressed in uniform, boots, and all. As she went outside and looked around, she realized that she was in France. Excited, yes, she was in Europe! France had been a dream and fantasy throughout her life, reading history books and romantic novels. Yet, here at the port, this certainly was not that literary vision. It was industrial, chaotic, and shrouded in thick industrial smog.

While the cargo and troops were transferred, Mazie, the handlers, and the cavalry troops all saw to the job of loading their animals. No sooner was the last animal loaded when she felt the train starting to move. She jumped from the equestrian car and started running alongside, keeping up with the quickening pace of the train. Out of breath, she leaped onto the troop car where she would be riding to her assigned duty station in the Champagne region northeast of Paris.

Tired as she might have been, she was in France and staring out the window, waiting for this beautiful country to take the shape of her fantasies. The villages, farms, and people were performing everyday tasks as if it were an enigmatic play. Mazie felt she was morphing into a character from a Rudyard Kipling novel Destination Unknown.

# Chapter 12

It was dawn, with barely enough light to work, as the train pulled into a remote station twenty miles west of Chateau-Thierry. Orders were given for all personnel to gather their belongings and fall out. Officers and Sergeants were barking orders for troops to assemble quickly and orderly onto a muddy, bumpy dirt road alongside the tracks. The last soldier stepped off the train, and man and beast scrambled to get ready to move on foot. Draft horses were first removed from the train and harnessed into teams of six horses to haul the equipment and cargo. Mazie moved up to the first car to assist with the unloading onto other platforms till all horses, mules, and donkeys had been safely unloaded. Mazie was amazed at how rapidly and organized the Cavalry troops were. They all lined up at the cars containing their saddles, then proceeded to locate their assigned steed, saddle up, and reassemble into formation. On adjoining platforms, were artillery guns, supply and cargo wagons, and ambulances, ready to be pulled by the horses, as soon as the motor vehicles got underway and out of their way.

The mounted cavalry moved toward the front, and led the mile-long procession. The newly erected Fort that they were heading to was a bombed champagne chateau that the British had been using.

* * *

The British had named it Fort Champagne after the once-grand estate known as the Chateau Beau Vignoble Champagne Vineyard in the Champagne Region of Northern France. Before the destruction of the war, the vineyard was an exquisite estate, rich with acres of Champagne grapes and endless fields of wildflowers. The grand old mansion was built in 1797. It was a two-story, U-shaped, luxurious stone manor. Ivy adorned the front and gothic stone elements. Arched windows with white window panes, and well-crafted rock walls and stone walkways lead up to the double wood-carved doors displaying fine skill and craftsmanship. Behind the house, the doux-Chateau had a large flower garden with an eight-foot-high rock privacy wall adorned with ivy, grass lawns, and carefully manicured hedges. Along the long side of the garden was an elegant building that served as an entertainment venue and tasting room.

Chateau Beau Vignoble covered five hundred acres, of which grew two-hundred and half of which were devoted to vines of the much desires Champagne grapes. Behind the now bombed main house were four fifty-foot by two-hundred-foot buildings, where the grapes were crafted and processed. The vintage was then barreled for two to five years until it was bottled, labeled, and ready to be stored in crates for worldwide export. There was a bombed and shattered greenhouse. Still intact were the support buildings for the champagne production, which included three bottling house and a three-car garage.

Also, an additional two-story, four-bedroom home once housed the winery's foremen, known as a Vigneron. The old, half-bombed-out main house of the Chateau exuded sadness, as it was a disgrace to see such a fine house that once housed the proud Chateau Beau Vignoble Champagne family.

Sadly, this former estate and vineyard had now been converted into a support depot by the English, with a triage hospital, veterinarian hospital, and offices. The Vigneron house was now the quarters for nurses and officers, and the four bombed out long buildings were made into stables, several corrals, and equipment storage spaces. Many, many rows of field tents to house the troops surrounded the adjoining area.

When they arrived at the fort, a small contingent of British troops was ready to assist the arriving Americans and help get them settled in. The British consisted of a few officers, a company of regular infantry, stable personnel, two nurses, a doctor, and an Australian veterinarian officer. The British had orders to stay for two weeks, so the Americans "CROWs", a British term for inexperienced soldier-or-Combat Recruit of War, would have time to settle in and establish a competent routine at the new Fort.

The British officers were in a strategic meeting with the American post command, filling them in on German troop movement past and present. Mazie was involved in a meeting with the British stable quartermaster and American soldiers responsible for horses and care for tack and rigging. When Mazie was introduced to the British, the younger ones thought it was some sort of a joke. However, the seasoned Brits who had served in India were not at all surprised, as they had employed the expertise of many East Indian horsemen.

A young Brit approached Mazie, stood two feet from her face, and said loudly, "Surely this is a joke. You are a little red skinned powwow princess. So, I am guessing, the Americans brought you along for a pleasure ride?"

Mazie could feel hatred and prejudice oozing out of his every pore. She responded, "Private, this war is hell. The only ride any of us should be thinking about is the ride to victory, then home, and hopefully not with our countries flag draped over us.."

A few of the younger Brits laughed while the men who had served in India kept a stern and serious face and were embarrassed by their comrades' rudeness. Their words had temporary value, as Mazie held her composure to a more serious note when she saw the American officers emerging from their meeting with the Brits, a look on their face as if they had all just been informed, they had terminal cancer.

Consequently, once they all saw her extraordinary skill with horses, it took just a few hours for the Brits to be in awe. In return, Mazie was quite impressed with the stables and entire facility the Brits had established from the war-torn buildings they had found and the additional ones they had built.

Off in the distance, before she could complete her walk back to the office, came the sound of multiple vehicles. The Brits did not take a defensive posture but scrambled to their duty stations to receive them. Even before the vehicles came to a stop, you could hear cries and screams of pain and anguish from the wounded as they pulled up to the triage hospital. Followed by two large trucks, who were rushing to the equine hospital.

Mazie ran to assist with the injured horses, but had no clue where to offer her help, as there were obvious procedures in place for unloading the horses and transferring them via mobile carts specifically designed to handle injured horses. She followed the last horse in and found an Australian Veterinarian. "Can I be of assistance, Sir? I have experience treating injured horses." Her mind flashed back to some of the horrible injuries horses and mules sustained at the mine back home.

Surprised that the question came from a woman's voice, the Veterinarian took a quick glance at the person behind the voice, he just heard. "Yes! Thank you,

Lieutenant. Could you please go out front and assist Sergeant Stephens with the Black gelding he is working on?" He quickly restored his concentration to the bleeding steed he was working on.

Mazie followed his instructions, introduced herself to Sergeant Stephens, triaged the black gelding, and then rushed off to the next casualty. Clearly, they were understaffed and had yet to make arrangements for an American Veterinarian to be assigned to this Fort. All but one of the horses had been moved into the treatment area except one, and the Sergeant asked Mazie to work on him. This horse was truly in pain, with a bad puncture wound in his front shoulder and a missing chunk of his hoof on the same leg. Mazie examined the horse only to discover the puncture wound was a gunshot wound. Upon further examination, she discovered that there was also an exit wound, eliminating the task of trying to remove a slug. Her knowledge of equine anatomy helped her to quickly determine that there was but minor damage done to the muscle, but she would have to stop the bleeding. There were enough instruments on the table near the horse for Mazie to start working. She quickly cleaned and then packed the wound to stop the bleeding. She then stitched both the entry and exit wound and wrapped it tightly with gauze and tape. She knew there wasn't anything she could do with the gelding's hoof, for it would grow back in time.

When the chaos had finally settled and horses had been cared for, she was tired, yet happy with how the horses were triaged. She went into the equine hospitable to say goodbye.

Proudly, she said, "Good night."

Both Sergeant Stephens and the Australian Major Thompson stopped to respond. "Lieutenant, thank you for your help," the Sergeant said.

Rubbing his shoulder that was in a sling, he beamed a big smile, and the Major extended his hand to Mazie and looked at her with respect. "Yes, Thank You, Lieutenant, I am grateful for your help today."

Mazie shook his hand and nodded her head in reply. And briefly, the Major and Mazie held each other's hand.

"Allow me to introduce myself. I am Major Thompson from the Australian Light Horse Cavalry." Letting go of the formality, "Please call me Walter."

Again, he shook Mazie's hand.

"Yes, Sir. Lieutenant Atencio, US Cavalry. But please call me Mazie," she said pridefully and walked out toward the stables.

Walter watched her as she walked back to the stables. "Ace, Isn't she a fine-looking Sheila?"

# Chapter 13

Located behind the once grand house of the Chateau Beau Vignoble were the still intact quarters of a two-story, four-bedroom home that formerly housed the Vigneron, which now housed the officers. The two bedrooms downstairs were occupied by the Forts Australian Veterinarian, Major Thompson, and Fort Champagne's British Commander, Lieutenant Colonel Niclas Jernigan, better known to all at Fort Champ as Nick the Dick. The two upstairs bedrooms were set up for Mazie and Adeline, the American nurse that Mazie had befriended on the ship. Mazie was grateful for her company and friendship. They spent many a night talking about life. Mazie had never had a close friend other than her brother Emiliano. Mazie was learning so much from Adeline, girly things she never had the opportunity to ask another woman.

Adeline told Mazie about being from Wisconsin and her life there. Mazie thought Adeline was a highly determined individual, so full of zeal that it made her stand out in a crowd. She had curly red hair, chubby cheeks, green eyes, big breasts, and a buxom figure and knew how to get men's attention. She was intelligent and always content with the knowledge that she was the best at what she did. She was also very good at helping others realize the quality of their work or the sheer persuasiveness of their personality. Most men desired her, and most women admired her.

To understand Adeline, one needed to get a glimpse of her background, which was so completely different from Mazie's. Adeline was from a small, charming picture-perfect community on the harbor of Lake Michigan in Port Washington, Wisconsin. She was raised by light housekeepers who operated the Saint Mary's Light Station built in 1860. Adeline's father, Hans Jones, was a mean and angry man with a wicked, uncontrollable temper. His wife Claire was a seventeen-year-old mail-away bride twenty years younger from Dingle, County Kerry, Ireland. It was a loveless marriage, and Hans physically and sexually abused Claire. He married Claire out of necessity to help him with the upkeep of the Light Station.

On the long voyage on the sailboat from Ireland, Claire made friends with a woman named Ida during the trip across the Atlantic. Ida was a huge masculine Irish woman-man, larger than most men; she was six foot four and weighed twice the weight of most men. On several occasions, Ida rescued Claire from the violating vulgar and perverted sexual advances of the ships drunken crew members.

Two years after Adeline was born, during a storm, Hans was at the top of the lighthouse, tending to the light, when a gust of wind blew him off the tower to his death, landing only twenty feet from Claire.

Claire kept the lighthouse operating for a year after Han's died. Claire needing help operating the lighthouse sought out Ida, who came to help maintain the Light Station and help to raise Adeline. The two worked together so compatibly that it blossomed into a relationship of personal fondness. So-called Christians took explicitly harsh and strict views of Lesbian love, and it was totally unexcepted and not tolerated. Yet Claire and Ida remained together. Their love for each other was never discussed at home, nor was it ever spoken of in the community. Adeline was raised in a house filled with love, light, and laughter and she loved her mother and Ida to no end.

* * *

During the first week at Fort Champagne, Mazie was so exhausted mentally and physically that she ate a late dinner and then went straight to bed. Every morning before she left her bed, she would talk to God and pray. She reminded herself within the prayer that we walk by the light of God. Getting on her knees, she prayed. "Dear God, you provide for me in so many ways, you have shown me that every question has your answer and every problem you can solve. When it is difficult to see my way through my day, I remember your light Dear God is always shining, illuminating the right and perfect path forward. The more I rely on my faith to show me the way, the brighter the guiding light gleams, allowing me a luminous path to start my day. Please continue to guide me Dear Lord, as I affirm that I will know, all I need, at the right and perfect time, pausing in prayer to listen to your guidance and awareness allowing my spirit to soar."

She then read a passage from her Bible. -Psalm 32:8 "I will instruct you to teach you the way you should go; I will counsel you with my eye upon you."

Mazie was still on her knees reciting Psalm when Adeline came into the room. "Oh! So sorry to interrupt you, Mazie."

"No… No… It's okay, please come in." Mazie sat on the bed.

Adeline had a weak smile, "I was never taught any prayers and never allowed at Saint Mary's church." Laughing. "So, there wasn't much religion in my upbringing."

Mazie recounted, "We didn't have a church in the town in which I lived. My father was raised Catholic. Being full-blooded Mimbres Indian, as a young child, my mother was forced to convert to Catholicism. My Aunts and Uncles from Mimbres told me several stories about how the Priests and nuns abused them. They also taught me the Mimbres faith and the strong connection between God and nature and that we shouldn't confuse religion with spirituality.

My father honored my mother's wishes not to make us go to church but to educate my brother and me on God's words through the spiritual teachings of the Bible."

"Your father sounds very wise."

Mazie felt comfortable with Adeline and said, "I feel that spirituality does not come from religion. I feel that it comes from our soul. I feel blessed to also know the spiritual traditions and teachings of the Mimbres people. Religion should not be looked upon as a set of rules, regulations, and rituals created by humans which were supposed to help people spiritually. But sadly, human imperfections have made religion corrupt, political, divisive, and a tool for power. Spirituality is not theology or ideology. It is a pure, simple way of life, and given to us only by the Great Spirit or what most people call God our Father."

"I admire your words and look forward to learning more from you," Adeline confessed.

Mazie offered her a warm smile and said "I would be happy and honored to share with you."

* * *

In the mid 1500's, when the Spaniards started to colonize New Mexico, Catholic priests forced the indigenous people into Catholicism. The Native American women, children, and the elderly who had been captured in warfare were forced to be converted to Catholicism, taught Spanish, and held in servitude by many New Mexican families. Over the years, the New Mexico territory changed hands from Spain, to Mexico, then in the early 20th century the United States.

Part of the church's effort in the 19th and 20th centuries was to gain mainstream acceptance in America. Numerous bishops and priests partnered with federal officials and their Protestant rivals in a shared project of forced assimilation of indigenous people, participating in family separations, and involuntary placement of Native American children in boarding schools where abuses regularly occurred.

In American Catholic history, many white Catholics of the Reconstruction Era and Gilded Age depicted Native Americans in racist, subservient ways. Historians argue that even when they had "the best of intentions, most missionaries failed to respect Indian cultures and spiritual beliefs, and traditions." They slandered indigenous cultures in attempts to fuse Catholicism and Americanism. And yet, many Native Americans remained devote to the Catholic faith and benefit from Catholic traditions.

President Ulysses S. Grant's description of indigenous people in his 1869 State of the Union message to Congress as "wards of the nation" represented a view shared by many white Catholics and Protestants. One Benedictine priest used identical language in 1893, describing "the Indian"' as "a spoiled child" and characterizing Native Americans as "the wards of the Nation, like overgrown children and minors." It was up to white Americans, the priest argued, to pull indigenous people out of their "filth and ignorance." Amazingly, he used these descriptors in the context of defending Native Americans from abuses perpetrated against them by the federal government and white settlers.

# Chapter 14

It had been a demanding day at Fort Champagne. Weary, fatigued, and dead-tired, Major Walter Andrew Thompson stumbled into his bedroom and eased himself down slowly onto his bed. He removed his arm from his sling and tried to relax and ease his discomfort. He took in several large cleansing breaths. But it was to no avail. He lay rubbing his aching shoulder. Even in his state of anguish, Walter was able to joke. "Crikey! It sure has been a long damn week, and its only Monday".

It only took him a few minutes to fall into a deep sleep. A sudden bolt of pain woke him from a ghastly nightmare. Walter was out of breath. He was covered with sweat, and his heart was trying to punch its way out of his chest. It took him several minutes to get his composure back. He realized that it was the same recurring nightmare that woke him when he was in the hospital recovering from a shrapnel wound received only months earlier at the Battle of Frommels.

Unable to get back to sleep, Walter's memory then took him back to when he was in the hospital. He recalled himself lying in the hospital bed, and he had tried to sit up, only to be hit with a blast of pain in his shoulder. The extreme jolt of pain quickly reminded him of how and why he was there. The pain had sucked out all of his youth. He sat up slowly and sat on the edge of his hospital bed. "Bloody awful. I am 25 years old, and I feel like Rip Van Winkle."

An old crotchety nurse came over to see if he needed help. He thought, "Has this poor woman ever smiled a day in her life?" He was trying his best to get a smile from her and said with his strong Australian accent, "I am so weak; a toddler could beat me up right now." The nurse's face seemed utterly expressionless. "Bloody hell, this woman is not very dag. She gives me the creeps," he thought. Another rush of pain surged through his body. In just the short amount of time he had been in the war, Walter had witnessed much pain, fatal catastrophes, and unthinkable human tragedy.

Some of the men in the nearby hospital beds overheard Walter's reaction to the mean nurse and were laughing at him. Walter was loved by many and hated by none. Walter continually put a lot of energy and care into his humor, which made him a star in his Brigade, and now he was a celebrity with his wounded buddies in the hospital.

* * *

The hours Walter spent recovering laying uncomfortably in his hospital bed did not allow him much sleep. One morning while sitting on the edge of his bed, he looked out the hospital window and saw a young lad sitting alone in the nearby field. The boy was crying. The boy appeared to be around 10 or 12. Seeing this young lad crying took him back to a memory of his own youth. He remembered sitting with his beloved elderly neighbor, BeeBee, while she held and embraced him.

Sobbing, he said, "Bee-Bee, I don't think my parents love me. I am nothing but a burden to them."

Bee-Bee sweetly said, "Walter, I know you didn't grow up with storybook role models. Life does not always deal us the right cards. But that doesn't mean you can't reshuffle your deck for a better outcome."


* * *


Walter was raised on a tiny family homestead in New South Wales, Australia, near the small town of Wagga Wagga. He learned most of his horsemanship and love for horses from the neighboring Aborigines and a widowed friend at a nearby horse ranch. He had twin sisters who were eight years older than him. Both sisters had married at a young age and moved away. His parents earned a low income and spent more time working on their small ranch than they did spending time with Walter.

Early in his youth, he befriended the wealthy widow neighbor, Beatrice Hutchins, owner and proprietor of the 4,222 square mile Hutchins Station. Walter had difficulty saying Beatrice's name, so he nick-named her Bee-Bee. Bee-Bee and Walter loved and cherished horses and shared countless hours working and training many steeds. Bee-Bee loved Walter as if he was her own. She never had children, so she doted on Walter to no end.

Bee-Bee set up Walter's own bedroom on the second story of her home. During his teenage years, Walter spent more time at Bee-Bee's station than at his parents' home. Unlike his stoic parents, Bee-Bee and Walter loved to laugh and joke together. Bee-Bee loved helping Walter with his school work which he continually excelled in. It seems that the only time Walter spent with his parents was on Sundays when they went to church, but even then, traditionally, he sat in the church pew next to Bee-Bee.

Beatrice knew she was living her final days and insisted that she pay for Walters College for veterinarian school in Sydney. It was only a few hours' ride back to Wagga Wagga, so he was able to continue to help Bee-Bee at her station during his downtime. Walter attended The University of Sydney School of Animal and Veterinarian Sciences, where he obtained his degree in Veterinarian Science and Doctorate in Veterinarian Medicine.

Walter's parents were not at his High School graduation, nor were they present at his graduation commencement from the University. And again, his parents were absent as his ship sailed off to War. But, Bee-Bee was there…

Walter was a beautiful man in so many ways. Not only was he attractive, but he had an infectious alluring, brilliant smile. He was an atlas of a man, strong and stalwart. But it was his gift of wit and unchanging kindness that was his acclaim.

*   *   *

The Australian commitment to the Great War began on August 4th, 1914, when the British Empire declared war on Germany and her allies. The young nation of Australia greeted the outbreak of the war with great enthusiasm. Australia's government and Prime Minister Andrew Fisher pledged their country's full support to their mother country, Britain.

Australia had no draft conscription. Amazingly, Australia had over four hundred thousand brave men who volunteered and enlisted for service in the Great War. Thirty-eight percent of the male population between the ages of eighteen and forty-four had volunteered from a population of less than five million to serve in the Great War. For Australia, the cost was high, with more than eight thousand seven hundred soldiers killed and eighteen thousand men wounded, gassed, or taken prisoner. In just eight months, a staggering amount of over fifty-six thousand Allied Troops died in the Battle of Gallipoli.

The Great War had already been in full force for a year when, in 1915, Walter enlisted in the Australian 9th Light Horse Regiment. Due to Walter's college education and Doctorate in Veterinarian Medicine, he entered as an officer and quickly moved up the ranks to Major once he had battlefield experience. The Light Horse Regiment, which Walter was a part of was a special group of mounted infantrymen and cavalry who traveled light and were well known for moving decisively from one combat zone to the other. They would ride their horses to the battlefield, dismount, and fight the battles from the ground.

The 9th Light Horse served and fought during the Gallipoli campaign, one of the their most terrifying battles in history. As well, hundreds of Native Australian Aboriginals, who were valued for working with horses and in hot climates, stepped up and fought as honored and heroic members of the Light Horse Regiment.

Unlike the Light Horse Mounted Regiment, the Australian regular cavalry faced the same horrid results as the French and British cavalry faced, that being the Turkish machinegun fire. Mounted and with swords drawn, they charged into battles resulting in mass genocide, as both men and horses were helplessly slaughtered and mowed down by machine gunfire.

From the beginning, Walter was quickly hardened from the battle of Gallipoli. The support troops from the 9th

Light Horse Regiment, including Shoe-Smiths, Farriers, Saddlers, and veterinarians, who all landed in Gallipoli in May 1915 were assigned to the care of the horses. Within eight months, Gallipoli was at a stalemate as the allies could not advance at the beach-head. The Turkish Army successfully held back the Australian and New Zealand Brigades, British Troops, and French Forces, all under the top-heavy, narcissistic British Command. Never would these combined allies make any progress, happenstance all withdrew.

After Gallipoli, Walter was sent to the front lines of Frommels, France. He had been wounded in the Battle of Frommels, where he took a nasty blow to the shoulder from artillery shrapnel while rescuing injured men and their horses. He was sent to a hospital in London to recover and received the British Star and The French Legion of Honor for his bravery in the battle. As soon as he was back on his feet, Walter was assigned to assist the British and newly arriving American troops occupying Fort Champagne in France.

# Chapter 15

A typical day at Fort Champagne consisted of Mazie getting up early to work with whichever horse needed her attention, and taking time out to teach the men who were assigned to her horse training techniques. Her men respected her and were honored that she shared her knowledge. Every day, she would notice a young boy sitting at the edge of the corral or stables watching her. Her curiosity finally got the best of her, so she rode the horse she was training over to the young lad. He had long, shaggy, uncombed black hair and brown eyes with a twinkle of blue in them. Strangely, he had a new inch-long cut on his cheek that was still healing into a scar. Even though he had very unkempt hair, he was surprisingly, very clean, and it was evident that he had outgrown his well-worn tattered clothes.

"Good morning, young man. I have seen you here for the past couple of days. Do you like horses?"

He rose up from sitting on the ground and stood tall. "Oui Mademoiselle. I love horses. But I do not know how to ride one."

Mazie dismounted the horse she was training and extended her hand. "My name is Mazie."

The young lad beams a huge smile and shakes Mazie's hand with a tight squeeze. "Me name is Remy."

"Gosh, with that strong handshake, you have the makings of a great horseman." Pointing toward the horse she was riding; she said this horse here doesn't have a name. Would like to name him for me."

"Oui, he looks like he should be named Hugo."

Mazie smiles. "Yes Remy, I think that Hugo is a perfect name for this horse."

Remy asks excitedly, "Are you an American Soldier? Are you here to get rid of those horrible Germans?"

"Yes, I am an American. And yes, all these troops are here to get rid of those nasty Germans."

Mazie questioned. "How old are you Mr. Remy?"

"I am eleven, but I am told I am wise for my age." Remy was very small for an eleven-year-old.

Mazie was enjoying talking to him. "Would you like to ride on this horse with me?

Remy gleamed, "Oui! Merci Mademoiselle Mazie, I would love to ride with you."

"Well, Remy there is one condition; that you call me Mazie." Lowering her tone, "You don't have to add Mademoiselle."

Mazie helped Remy onto the horse and sat him behind her. "Put your arms around me, and hold on."

As horse and riders rode around the corral for several minutes. Remy was enjoying his ride with Mazie. Remy askes "Mazie, will you teach me how to ride as good as you?"

"I would love to Remy. Horses are incredible gifts from God. Those who teach us the most about life are not always humans." They rode for several minutes before returning back at the stables.

Mazie lowered Remy to the ground, then dismounted. Concerningly, Mazie asks, "I hope your parents don't mind that I took you on a ride."

The boy suddenly became very sad. "No, Mazie, they would not have minded."

Mazie's concern for the boy deepens. "Where do you live Remy?"

"Over there," Remy answered, pointing toward the north. And he quickly changed the subject. "Me Papa used to work in the vineyard here at Chateau Beau Vignoble before the Germans blew it up."

"Would you like to come with me to the mess tent to get something to eat?" Looking at the boy, it appeared as if had been several days since he had a good meal.

His smile reappeared. "Oui, Mazie. Merci! Merci!"

As they were leaving the stables, Major Thompson came escorting a mare. "Good morning, Lieutenant Atencio I was hoping that I would catch you. Would you or one of your men please take some time with this mare today? She had colic and I think she needs light exercise. Nothing strenuous, just keep her moving"

"We'd be happy to help Major," Mazie replied.

"And who is this young lad?" Walter said with a smile, messing Remy's hair.

"Me name is Remy, Sir."

Mazie added, "Remy informed me that his family home was to the north. And that his father used to work here when this was a working vineyard."

Remy just nodded his approval.

Mazie called out to one of her men to lightly exercise the mare and gave him the reins to lead the horse into the corral.

Walter pointed at the wooden wall of the stables. The wood was primitively cut and still had its bark on it. He teased Remy, "Hey Remy Little Mate, do you know why the wood here is called dogwood?"

"No, I do not know." A puzzled Remy replied.

Walter laughed out the answer, "Because it has bark on it!"

Remy thought about it for a few seconds, then busted out in laughter. "Dog Wood. That's funny!"

Mazie was laughing too. "Major, Young-Remy and I were just going to the mess tent to get a quick lunch. Would you care to join us?"

"Ace! That's where I was going next. I would love to join you."

As the three walked to the mess tent Walter continued to tease Remy. "So, Remy you liked my joke about Bark and Dog Wood?"

Beaming he agreed, "Yes, Sir."

"I know I was going out on a limb with that joke." Laughing, "I was afraid you would want me to "leaf" after that joke." Adding, "Why aren't you rooting for me?"

Mazie and Remy laughed the entire way to the mess tent.


Walter, Mazie, and young Remy sat together in the Mess tent while the camp cook, Big Bean, went to make them something special for their late lunch. Big Bean was a British Saff Sergeant in charge of Fort Champagnes food service. Big Bean was a gentle giant with big dreams of becoming a Chef when the war ended.

Adeline came in for a cup of coffee and sat with them. Mazie introduced her to Remy.

Walter then cheered with celebration, "I'd like to make a toast to our new little friend, Remy."

Remy's eyes lit up and he smiled fondly.

Walter, Mazie, and Adeline clinked their coffee mugs to Remy's glass of milk. "Cheers!" they all chimed in.

Walter teased, "Remy, why do our fingers have fingertips? But our toes don't have toetips?"

Remy giggled. "I don't know."

During their lunch together Mazie tried to get some more information out of Remy as to who he was and about his family. But he was being secretive. Just then a courier from the Army came in. He spoke out. "I was told that I could find Lieutenant Atencio here."

Surprised that he was asking for her, she stood up. "I am Lieutenant Atencio."

"I have a telegram for you Ma'am." The Private was equally surprised when he found she was a woman.

Mazie had never had a telegram before and became concerned. She read it slowly.

*Western Union Telegram*

*To: Mazie Atencio.*

*From: Spencer Penrose Jr.*

*Mazie Atencio. This is to inform you on this day of July 19th, the year of 1917, Petitioner Spencer Penrose Jr. has filed for divorce at the Judicial District Court, County of Grant, State of New Mexico. Upon review of the court, the Honorable Joseph G. Harrington has granted the Divorce Decree. The Divorce between Petitioner Spencer Penrose Jr. and Respondent Mazie Atencio has been granted, and filed, releasing both parties of any marital obligations.*

Everyone sitting around Mazie sat quietly watching Mazie's face and seeing what the telegram news said. At first, Mazie was stern-faced until she reread it, and her face lit up with relief. She released a big sigh! She looked up at the staring faces around her. "Oh! It is okay. Yes, it is good news. Wonderful news." She didn't give anyone any explanation. She just folded the telegram and put it in her pocket.

* * *

Remy stayed in the mess tent to play cards with Big Bean. As Mazie and Walter were leaving the tent, an entourage of six Army motor cars followed by an endless parade of M-1917 Light American Model Tanks came riding into camp. The noise they were making was deafening. Mazie wanted to put her hands over her ears. In the lead vehicle Mazie noticed Captain George Patton. At the same time, Captain Patton saw Mazie and signaled his driver toward her. Captain Patton got out of the car and made his way over to Mazie. "Well, Lieutenant Atencio, you are just the person I was looking for." He shook Mazie's hand sternly.

"Lieutenant Patton, it is good to see you, Sir." Surprised by his visit she didn't know what to say.

He pointed at his epaulets on the shoulder of his crisply pressed uniform. "Lieutenant Atencio, I have made the rank of Captain, since I last saw you."

Again, Mazie shook his hand, "Congratulations Sir." Adding, "Sir, I did not know you were here in France."

"Yes, yes… I am, but only for a short time. Then who knows where my commanding officer will send me, could be the coast or could be the front."

Mazie spoke with confidence. "May I introduce to you Major Thompson of the Australian Light Horse Brigade. Major Thompson is our veterinarian here at Fort Champagne."

The two shook hands. Walter greeted the captain. "Proud to know you, Captain Patton."

The three momentarily talked about the Fort, the Cavalry units, and the horses. Patton then informed Mazie. "Lieutenant, I need you to help me with a matter of importance. You see, your wonderous reputation with horses has far-far proceeded you. The honorable French Stateman George Clemenceau, who is serving as the Prime Minister of France his, "God-Daughter", as he called her, Therese Juliette, has requested that you take a look at her prize Arabian Stallion. They have already had several horse professionals look at him and I would greatly appreciate your expertise"

"Major Thompson, now that I've made your acquaintance, I will request that you go along with Lieutenant Atencio." Clearing his throat he added, "Major Thompson and Lieutenant Atencio, I realize that it is a bunch of malarkey. However, with France embroiled in a bitter war, it is imperative that we maintain our relations with our allies."

Captain Patton then filled them in with more information and he would arrange for them to leave for Paris the following week. Concluding, Caption Patton added, "The Noblesse au premier degreé, St. Andre Gatineau, and his wife Therese Juliette, will send their private motor-car to pick you up."

Captain Patton proceeded to tell them the story of the French Prime Minister George Clemenceau and his soon to be wife.

The love between Minister George Clemenceau, and the American Mary Plummer began in 1868.

It's hard to believe that the small-town girl, Mary Plummer, from little ole Skinner's Prairie, Michigan led an ostentatious, glamorous life as the spouse of the Prime Minister of France. But the fate and kismet of her beauty led her to courtship as in Connecticut, with George Clemenceau. Mary Plummer was born to William T. Plummer and Harriet in Springfield, Massachusetts, in 1849.

Her father became ill and in 1857 moved his family out west, where they settled in the town of Durand, Michigan. In 1860, William Plummer died leaving his wife Harriet to raise Mary, her brother Will, and sister Susie alone. Thankfully, four years later, 1864, when Mary was 15, her mother's brother and his wife, Mr. and Mrs. Horace Taylor, came for a visit. When her uncle realized how beautiful Mary was, he offered to educate her at the Catherine Aiken Seminary in Stamford Connecticut. Mary adapted quickly to the highly glamorous clothes of the era. She had been dressed plainly throughout her life and wore the new clothes with natural grace and poise, refining her beauty.

While teaching French at the seminary, Mary's beauty caught the attention of Professor George Clemenceau, and romance developed quickly. George Clemenceau was known as a very bizarre teacher, very peculiar and yet very artistic. A whirlwind romantic courtship took place, and in less than a year, the twenty-year-old Mary Plummer wed the twenty-eight-year-old George Clemenceau in June of 1860, in New York City Mr.

and Mrs. Clemenceau moved to Castle L'Aubray in the Vendees in France.

The highly educated George immediately entered politics, and in 1870, Clemenceau was elected Mayor of the French Village of Montmarte and soon after became a member of the French National Assembly. As he became more powerful, his loving marriage to Mary dissolved until George denied that he had ever known or loved Mary. His power had overcome his love for her, however, he wished for a divorce. However, they never did annul the marriage for fear that the divorce would ruin his theocracy, reputation, and thus his career in politics. Yet, as the Germans continued to push further into France, Clemenceau offered to provide sanctuary for Mary and their two daughters.

Mary declined the offer along, with pleas from relatives in the United States to return to her family. She decided to move to Paris and left the Castle in Vendees with only a few belongings and clothes to start a new life. Though George abundantly provided for his two daughters, Mary lived a conformable life and worked. Over the years spent in Paris, she worked as a gallery guide for American tourists and wrote articles for American magazines. Their oldest daughter, Madeleine, became a famous newspaper writer and speaker. Daughter Therese remained in touch with her father George Clemenceau even though he publicly denied his fatherhood of her. Yet, George spoiled Therese and spent thousands of l'argent on her high society wedding.

Therese Juliette led the life of a queen when she married St. Andre Gatineau. They had one son, William Benjamin, who presently held the position of colonel in the French army. Juliette and Andre lived a life of great wealth and flaunted their glamorous lifestyle. Juliette loved horses and was well known for her selective Arabian breeding.

# Chapter 16

Noblesse au premier degreé, St. Andre Gatineau, and his wife Therese, Juliette Gatineau, greeted Walter and Mazie as they entered the ostentatious parlëure. Neither Mazie nor Walter had ever stepped into a house so grand.

The house was an artistically-designed Tudor-style manor that sat in the middle of twenty forested acres to the west of Paris. Built-in 1898 using a white limestone block typical of the region, it had an impressive eight step stone staircase that ascended from the perfectly manicured landscaped courtyard to the main entrance.

The grand house opened into a great entry with wide-plank oak floors, high ceilings with eclectic carved wooden beams, and an intricately detailed wooden carved staircase with a copious floor-to-ceiling stained-glass window.

The three-story house had a grand room with a decorative fireplace, an office and library, and two kitchens; a cellar garde manger kitchen and a kitchen on the main floor, an open two-story dining room, and two sitting parlors. Limestone steps led up to nine en-suite bedrooms, each with a stylish bathroom, dressing room, and balconies. And the most modern of all, it had electricity throughout the house.

Brief introductions were made by Andre and Therese, and their Maître Buttiler was summoned to show Walter and Mazie to their guest quarters.

The back of the house was well landscaped around the surrounding century-old sequoia and oak trees, including several outbuildings; including a guest house that was the original house built in 1781; two barns; and stone-built stable that housed twelve overpriced horses.

Next, Walter and Mazie were given a tour of the stables, where they were introduced to the cause for their visit, a four-year-old Arabian named Maurice Afires Heir, more affectionately known as le Capitaine. Le Capitaine was a striking bay stallion with a beautifully exquisite dished face, sleek, elegant body, and high tail carriage. He held an iconic rich color and conformation, giving him an elegant look of a prestigious pedigree.

When Mazie was younger, she became fascinated with Arabians when she first saw one on display in the Plaza in Silver City. She asked its owner continual questions about the steed, until he brushed her off for being bothersome. She then read and studied about the notorious horse breed.

As Le Capitaine was led out to the stable courtyard, he immediately reared up with his disapproval. It took several men to hold his lead rope while several more men stood away from him in fear. Mazie waited until Le Capitaine was settled down a bit. Slowly, and calmly, she walked up to his side so he could get the full view of her. In a hushed tone, she pointed out to the stablemen.

"You must stay completely calm when you are around him. And do not stand directly in front of him, because he cannot see you. Stay off to the side of his head. Horses' eyes are on the side of their heads and cannot see directly in front of them. Some Arabians have smaller skulls than most horses, so their site is even more obstructed."

Walter stepped in to add a further explanation. "Horses have a field of vision which is approximately 146 degrees for each eye, which allows them a panoramic view around them, yet a narrow blind spot directly in front and behind them."

Mazie gently took the steeds lead rope and with a soft hypnotic voice, sedately spoke to the horse in her native Mimbres language.

"It is vitally important to understand his behavior before you start handling or training Le Capitaine. Because there are distinct genetics and differences in this breed of horse."

Looking around at the stable hands, "Which of you feel most comfortable working with Le Capitaine?"

"Oui, Mademoiselle I do." He was a small, stocky man with flaming red hair."

What      is      your      name      sir?"

"Mademoiselle, they call me Rousseau."

"I suggest that only Rousseau work with Le Capitaine until he becomes calmer and more relaxed around people. This will not happen fast, so you all need to be patient."

"Keep in mind that it is instinctual for any stallion to have to be the head of the herd, even if it's in a barn or stables. Keep him away from other stallions, or three or more mares in a group."

She stopped to pet the noble steed's forehead, then continued her instructions. "Arabians naturally enjoy the company. When other female Arabians are not present, they usually bond with horses, mules, ponies, burros, or other small stock such as goats. I recommend you find him a full-time companion such as a goat, small female horse, or a gelded pony, or burro. Due to their territorial nature, slowly introduce **Le Capitaine to his** livestock companion, and this must be supervised. However, **Le Capitaine** could develop a powerful bond with his companion, and separating the bonded pair can create enough stress to result in a serious sickness that can be fatal. It is imperative that everywhere **Le Capitaine goes, his companion must go with** him."

Now directing her words to **Rousseau.** "Every time you interact with an Arabian, they will learn something.

During learning, an Arabian doesn't consider their behavior good or bad, only whether this new learning affects them. How any horse is trained and handled will determine their behavior. An experienced trainer who communicates well will help a horse to overcome problems and learn more rapidly than a horse with an impatient or inexperienced handler. The stoic and hard-to-read Arabians' body language is often less expressive than most horse breeds, and so a change in their behavior may be subtle. A slight widening of the eyes might be misread as an increased curiosity when it could actually mean fear or stress. A lack of movement away from a fearful object can easily be misread as confidence rather than the Arabian's reduced flight response. The better you get to know this horse and what is usual for them, the easier it will be to spot these subtle changes."

"Monsieur St. Andre Gatineau and Mademoiselle Therese Juliette Gatineau have brought Major Thompson here to check Le Capitaine to make sure he doesn't have any physical problems that are causing him pain or causing him to act out and, of course, the pain causing his misbehavior." Mazie stood back and let Walter examine the horse.

Walter stepped in, "Good on ya, Rousseau, for stepping in to help with this magnificent animal." He then addressed the group. "What Lieutenant Atencio is referring to with Le Capitaine's strong bond with his companion and separating the bonded pair can create enough stress to result in the serious condition of hyperlipemia."

Later, after Walter checked over Le Capitaine, he affirmed that he was in excellent health.

With nerves of steel, Mazie cooed, charmed, and pacified the horse. Within hours, she was up riding Le Capitaine in an inspiring calm, trot. The horse trainers for Le Capitaine were in total awe as they witnessed the remarkable tranquil horsemanship of this native American girl. Mazie worked well into the night with Le Capitaine and his newly assigned personal trainer, Rousseau. She then met them early in the morning and continued the training of both horse and trainer Rousseau. When she witnessed Rousseau's progression with Le Capitaine she knew she had helped.

Walter wandered over to where the other handlers watched Mazie and Rousseau in awe. "Mates, now you know why they call her "Horse Girl" hey?"

To show their gratitude, Monsieur St. Andre Gatineau and Therese Juliette Gatineau offered Mazie and Walter to stay in their guest house for as long as they needed. And offered for their personal chauffeur to take them wherever they wanted in Paris. Mazie and Walter knew they would have to return to Fort Champagne within two days and wanted to take the opportunity to pick up supplies while in Paris.

Walter and Mazie introduced themselves to the chauffeur at the beginning of the tour. They learned his name was Guillaume Sotheby's, and they all agreed for each of them to go on a first-name basis. Not only did they learn that Guillaume was a family man with five children, they learned that he had never taken a tour of the Eiffel Tower, he had only visited the Norte Damn cathedral, so Walter and Mazie convinced him to join them.

Guillaume explained that the Eiffel Tower is located at the river-Seine, where the river divides the city into two halves, called the Left Bank and Right Bank. The right bank is on the north side, left to the south. The right bank claimed to represent Paris's sophistication and modern development, while the left bank has the universities, parks, and historic areas.

The immense structure of the Eiffel Tower was a wrought-iron lattice tower on the Champ de Mars in Paris, France. It is named after the engineer Gustave Eiffel, whose company designed and built the tower for the 1889 World's Fair. Then soon, it would become the ultimate symbol of Paris.

Guillaume further explained the Eiffel Tower was almost torn down in 1909 at the expiration of its twenty-year lease but was saved because of its antenna — used for telegraphy. Beginning in 1910 it became part of the International Time Service. It has been built to celebrate the science and engineering achievements of its age, soaring 984 feet and 1,052 feet including the antenna, and weighed 7000 tons. The structure consisted of two visibly distinct parts; a base composed of a platform resting on four separate supports called pylons. Above this, a slender tower was created as it tapered upward, rising above a second platform to merge in a unified column.

This unprecedented work, the tallest structure in the world, had several antecedents. Among them were the iron-supported railway viaducts designed by Eiffel, an arch bridge over the Douro River in Portugal with a span of 525 feet, and a design for a circular, iron-frame tower proposed by the American engineers Clarke and Reeves for the Centennial Exposition of 1876. Gustave Eiffel knew and publicly acknowledged this influence; he was no stranger to the United States, having designed the wrought-iron pylon inside Frederic Bartholdi's Statue of Liberty in 1885.

However as tricky as its birth may have been, the Tour Eiffel was now wholly accepted by French citizens and has now become internationally recognized as one of the symbols of Paris itself.

Walter, Mazie, and Guillaume started their exploration in the basement of the Eiffel towers eastern and western pillars. They visited the gargantuan 1899 machinery which powered the elevators. It had been the first time taking an elevator for the trio, and soon enough, they discovered the top of the tower, which provided an astonishing view of the city of Paris. It was a breathtakingly superb site to see. From the top, they could see below them the Trocadéro fountains that were in full force and watched the performances around the Palais de Chaillot, which was filled with dancers and acrobats. Off in the distance, they could see the vast green esplanade of the Parc du Champs-de-Mars. Formal lawns of the 18th-century École Militaire-

Military Academy, where their well-manicured formal lawns displayed the parade ground for French troops.

Returning to the plaza grounds they encountered an organ grinder with a monkey, some drummers, musicians, and artists on the Quai de Conti. Wandering into the Eiffel Towers Le Péage-Plaza, the three ate lunch at a nearby café, where they had the favored croque monsieur or croque madam, a toasted cheese sandwich with ham. Neither Walter nor Mazie had ever had pizza so the two shared a slice of the popular Italian pizza Paris-style.

As if seeing one of the most iconic monuments in the world wasn't enough to fulfill their Parisian afternoon fantasy, Walter, Mazie, and Guillaume hurried over to the swirl-and-whirl at the Carousel of the Eiffel Tower. Carousels are very popular in Paris. The French word for carousel is *manège,* which is more akin to the merry-go-round.

Mazie was so excited. "I have read about carousels. Let's go ride it! Can we please?"
Walter laughed. "Ace Mate, let's ride the carousel." Laughing, he added, "Sometimes I question my sanity, but the unicorn in my bedroom told me that I'm fine."

Mazie and Guillaume laughed at Walters's adage.

Guillaume claimed, "I'll let the two of you ride the carousel."

Walter teased Guillaume, "Oh come join us."

Guillaume laughed, and shook his head no.

Proud of himself Walter added, "Some people are afraid to be corny. Not me. I like life on the cob."

Mazie of course, chose the white horse to ride, and Walter was next to her on a camel.

"Look, Walter, I am riding a white steed like my horse at the fortt, Hercules." It had been many years since she felt the kid-at-heart in herself.
Walter watched Mazie and thought to himself. Ace! She is truly a beautiful woman, both inside and out. He sighed, thinking, damn this war. I wish we were in better circumstances so I could get to know her better.

The carousel was built in 1913 and was located directly across the street from the Eiffel Tower. It was indeed a piece of art, a wonderous attraction with hand-sculpted wooden horses sculpted by the famous Limonaire brothers. The roof depicted stunning artwork of Paris; as it turned, you could take a delightful trip with its landscapes, colors, gardens, and nature. It was Paris in a panoramic version, a Manège jeu de bagues.

* * *

Due to the war and the current location of the German front line being only 40 miles away, the Palace of Versailles was closed to visitors. The Louver Museum had removed all the precious art pieces which were then safely stored in the city of Toulouse. So, their next stop was a brief visit to Notre-Dame de Paris, which means, "Our Lady of Paris", referred to simply as Notre-Dame. It was a Medieval Catholic cathedral on the Île de la Cité-Island in the Seine River, in the 4th arrondissement of Paris.

The cathedral, dedicated to the Virgin Mary, is considered one of the finest examples of French Gothic architecture. Several attributes set it apart from the earlier Romanesque style, particularly its pioneering use of the rib vault and flying buttress, enormous and colorful rose windows, and the naturalism and abundance of it sculptural decoration.

Construction of the cathedral began in 1163 under Bishop Maurice de Sully was primarily completed by 1260, and was continually modified in the succeeding centuries. In the 1790s, during the French Revolution, Notre Dame suffered extensive desecration: much of its religious imagery was damaged or destroyed.

Mazie couldn't believe that humans could destroy such a work of beauty.

Guillaume took the role of their tour guide through the cathedral as Walter and Mazie "Ooh'ed and Ah'ed" their way through the magnificent conventicle. Both Walter and Mazie stopped to say a silent prayer before leaving.

Guillaume took out his pocket watch and warned the two, "We'd better be heading out if you want to pick up your supplies."

Walter joked, "Darn where is my pocket watch? I was going to look for my missing watch… But the time got away from me."

It was a fabulous day all around; neither Walter nor Mazie wanted for it to end, but they had supplies to pick up, and Guillaume then took them back to Fort Champagne.

# Chapter 17

Back at Fort Champagne, it was business as usual. Mazie stayed busy training horses, Walter returned to the mending and care of horses and minor wounds of the troops.

Remy came to visit Mazie as always, but today, he was in a strange mood, somber and subdued. "Mazie, can I borrow Hercules this morning to help me move something back home? I won't ride him. I'll just lead him like you taught me. I know he is your favorite horse, and I promise to take care of him and bring him right back."

This was a strange request, Mazie thought. "Can I come to help you, Remy? Does your Papa need our help?"

He quickly snapped, "Oh no, Mazie, I… ah… we don't need your help. I… ah… we can do it ourselves, honest."

"Okay Remy. Let me help you harness up Hercules." This was very odd. What was Remy up to?

She harnessed up Hercules and handed the lead rope to Remy. "You sure you don't need our help."

Remy just shook his head no when he walked off into the woods. She watched and smiled at the site of Remy next to that giant white horse. Her smile soon turned to concern.

Walter stopped by to bring Mazie supplies and noticed Remy walking into the woods, leading Hercules.

"Walter, something strange is going on with Remy. He said he needed to use Hercules to move something on his farm. There is something peculiar about his request. And I've never seen Remy in such a cloudy mood."

Suddenly worried, Walter said, "Let's follow him and see what he is up to. As much as we love that little Mate, he has kept us all in the dark far too long, and it's time we meet his parents don't you think?"

Mazie agreed. Walter quickly saddled up a horse, and Mazie jumped on a horse bareback and the two followed Remy for over a mile through the woods. A well-beaten path that led them right to the old farmhouse where they found Remy. He had a rope tethered to Hercules and was leading Hercules to haul off a dead rotten mule.

Remy was so surprised to see Walter and Mazie that he started to cry when they came near him. "Please don't tell anyone."

Mazie and Walter got down off her horse. Mazie reassured him in a sweet tone. "It's okay Remy. Why don't you tell Walter and I what is happening here." Her heart was filled with exquisite tenderness.

Remy ran over to Mazie and started sobbing so hard he couldn't speak. Mazie sat down on the ground wrapping her arms tightly around Remy. "You are all right Remy. Everything is fine."

Walter came and sat next to them and joined in on the hug. The three sat for minutes, hugging and holding each other until Remy had calmed down and was able to speak.

Trying to control his crying so that he could speak, he managed to say, "Please don't send me to an or-fig-nage."

Mazie quickly figured out what he was trying to pronounce. "No Remy don't worry sweet boy. Take your time and tell us what happened."

Walter sweetly patted Remy on the back. "You will be okay. little Mate."

Trying to sound brave, Remy said. "A couple of months back, the Germans came and shot me Mama and me Papa. I had been out in the woods chasing one of our chickens that got loose, so they didn't see me."

He began a flood of tears and sobbed, "The Germans killed my parents and shot our mule. They took our chickens and two cows." He was wailing so hard he shook and shuddered uncontrollably and couldn't catch his breath.

Walter grabbed Remy and laid him down. "Catch your breath little Mate. Breath…"

Tearing up, Mazie was so overwhelmed by the site of Remy's storming emotions. "Remy, you are fine. We will take care of you… Take a deep breath, Remy."

After Remy's breathing turned back to normal, Mazie picked up Remy laid him in her arms, and rocked him. Walter, stayed next to them, rubbing his shoulders and legs.

Walter realized that what Remy was trying to do was remove the dead, rotting corpse of their mule. He used Hercules to pull the mule off into the woods and returned.

"It took me a long time to dig two graves and bury me Mama and me Papa over there." Remy pointed to two graves near the garden. Mazie please don't let them put me in an or-fig-nage, please? I have heard horrible things about that place."

Mazie's mind raced back to the stories her cousins in New Mexico had told her about the Catholic nuns kidnapping the native American children and forcing them to live in the orphanage.

"You will be fine Remy. Walter and I will see what we can do to help you."

"Not to worry little Mate," Walter reassured him again. "I cannot believe you have been out here alone for the last several months. You are a strong young man. I'm proud of you."

* * *

Remy told stories of his life before the war and what hardworking people his wonderful parents were. He told them the disgusting details of how he watched his parents shot in the back as they ran for cover from the invading German soldiers. And that the soldiers laughed as they shot them.

Later, Walter, Mazie, and Remy returned to the Camp, where they took Remy to Walter's quarters to get some rest and figure out what they would to do for the boy.

Sergeant Stephens was Walter's right-hand man and Walter trusted and admired him. "Sergeant Stephens, will you please set up a cot in my quarters and see that Remy is comfortable?"

Shaking his head, Walter let out a big sigh. "Sergeant, how many children did you tell me you had?"

"Major, I have three children: one girl and two boys."

Still shaking his head, Walter added. "Make sure you teach your children to be good friends to other children. Because not all of them have a loving home to go home to."

* * *

Everyone at the Fort cared for Remy and within the next couple of days, everyone teamed up to support and look out for him.

A week later, Maize received her first letter from her brother Emiliano, informing her that their papa had passed away. Heartbroken as she was, she knew she had to finish getting four horses ready for a small Cavalry reconnaissance unit scheduled to leave early that afternoon. She kept herself busy to keep her mind off of the letter containing the dispirited news of her father passing.

When the cavalry unit left, Mazie harnessed up Hercules and rode bareback into the woods. She rode for several miles with Hercules at a full run with full fury. She climbed up to a grassy ridge. In getting to the top, she suddenly had to stop, or she would fall into a big open pit. Hercules reared up from the force of the sudden stop. Both horse and riders' breath bellowed from exertion. The horrendous smell that suddenly filled her nostrils made her look further out at what was in the large pit below. It was a gruesome unbelievable site. The three-hundred-foot round pit, was filled with dead decomposing, carcasses of horses and mules. There were dozens of vultures feasting on the carcasses. The horrific site before her, along with the putrid smell of death, sent her into delirium. Four years of battle in this area of France had massacred dozens of horses, which had been thoughtlessly tossed into an open grave.

She turned Hercules around, in a storm, she hurried down the ridge so furiously that most riders would have plummeted to the ground. When she got to a flat area, she slid off Hercules and frantically examined her mind for what she had just witnessed. Her mind was stained from the ghastly site of the sea of dead horses. As she mentally continued to uncoil, she suddenly realized why she had taken this ride. It was because of the death of her father. Mazie sank to the ground onto her knees and cried out loudly in sorrowful anguish. She screeched with madness as her soul screamed in a tremendous, wild rage. Her body shook as it was overtaken by vehemence and nausea swept over her. She bent forward and vomited.

In a depth of misery, Mazie sat and screamed, only baffled by the thunderhead of tears, until her tears settled into sorrows and calmed her heavy heart.

The evil destruction of this war and the noxious death that it rained was overwhelming. The sinister quality of it all crept over her like a thousand worms. Mazie could not fathom how and why mankind could allow history to continually repeat unutterable massacre through war. She called out to the heavens, "Wake up people. If we are not at peace with each other, it only means that we don't understand each other." There was a pain in her chest that merged with her soul. She pulled herself up from the dark, and then cried until she could not cry anymore.

Softly, she whimpered, "Father God, please bring peace to your people."

This simple message to God made her smile weakly as she remembered her papa telling her, "Peace starts in our own minds and hearts, and when the root of peace is firmly entrenched in ourselves, we then start to share it with our community, and the whole wide world."

Remembering this, she added to her prayer. "And Dear God, wrap a blanket of peace around me… Cover this land with a blanket of peace… Wrap a loving blanket of peace around the world..." Her faithful companion Hercules sensed that Mazie was in despair, came over to her, and nudged her. Mazie thanked him for his love and patted him while she sat on the ground crying.

She called out to the sky, "Papa, enjoy heaven. And just know that you have left a legacy of love and peace for everyone whom you knew while here on this earth." Tearing up again, she whimpered, "I love you, Papa."

She lay on the ground staring up at the sky for several hours. Deciding she better get back to the Fort, she let out a huge cleansing sigh and called out to the heavens, "Lord, I know the blood of the innocent does not lie idle and that it calls out to man for vengeance. Lord, end the shedding of innocent blood around the world. Destroy the schemes of the wicked who hunger for war and power. Quench the insatiable fire of the greedy and murderous people will not inherit Your kingdom in heaven.

Remembering scripture, she recited, Isaiah 26:3. "Thou wilt keep him in perfect peace, whose mind is stayed on thee: because he trusteth in thee. When God swallows up death forever."

"Please, Dear God, never leave my side. Carry me in your protective hands. Let all that I do bring glory to you. Take me through today with grace, peace, and protection."

# Chapter 18

It was unnerving for Mazie to listen to the gunfire as she worked with the mules in the corral. It was a morning filled with storming bursts of gunfire, booms and echoes, and thuds that continued to roar throughout the land to the north. The dull booms reminded her of an erratic heartbeat from a beast. She had spent several hours that morning training the four mule teams to get them accustomed to their harnesses because the mule teams would be heading to the front in the morning to haul more supplies and ammunition. Work harnesses built for strength and durability included steel hardware. Total gear and harness weight ranged from one hundred fifty to two hundred pounds each.

Remy showed up adorning his usual bright smile. He came eagerly, wanting to learn how all the harnesses work. "Good morning, Miss Mazie."

Mazie bent down to give Remy a hug. "Good morning." Releasing a sigh, she said. "Remy, I am almost finished up here and I'm tired of listening to the gun fire to the north of us. What do you say we take Hercules for a quick ride to the south, away from all the gunfire?"

"I would like that." He nodded.

Mazie and Remy rode through the countryside, Remy sat behind Mazie, holding onto her. Remy chatted breathlessly the entire ride asking Mazie about American Indians. To amuse him, she made up a war-cry to teach him. A few miles out they found a quiet place, were they laid back and settled in on a grassy slope, looking up at the sky. "Isn't the sky beautiful? Don't you wish you could kiss the sky?" She blew a kiss up to the heavens. Remy laughed and did the same.

With a quizzical look, Remy looked at Mazie, and asked. "Mazie how is it that horses like you so much? It's like you have some kind of horse magic."

Mazie laughed and smiled. "My people, the Native Americans, are well known for their horsemanship. Our people tell many stories and legends about instinctive skills and spiritual agreements with horses. The key to training horses is one's ability to become "one-with" as a horse and rider. You need to have a natural kinship and understanding of horses, allowing the rider to communicate and connect with horses on a deep level. The rider should use a combination of body language, vocal cues, and an understanding of equine behavior to build trust and rapport with the horse. You must create a calm and harmonious spiritual energy with the horse. The rider needs to establish a respectful and cooperative relationship between the human and horse based on mutual trust and understanding.

Remy snarled his nose. "Huh! Explain, please."

"A rider's ability to communicate with horses can be remarkable". Mazie went on to tell Remy, "Being 'one-with' is my essential belief. My people have lived with the understanding that people must trust and be one with their environment, one with God's creatures, and one with Mother Earth. That included one with the sun, moon, and stars. And most importantly, we must be one with God, our creator. Trust is an essential part of being 'one-with'. Most animals are born with the understanding to trust everything until there is a reason not to trust. It does not take much to lose a horse's trust.

The basics of trust when training a horse is to use calmness and kindness rather than domination. You must use the appropriate body language when you give commands, observe your horse and listen to him by learning to interpret his behavior.

Acting as 'one-with' with your horse is the most sought-after skill of riders of all equestrian disciplines at all levels. It requires open, two-way communication between horse and rider. Becoming "one-with" a horse can easily be gained, but by no means does it come quickly. To assure a true partnering relationship and establish open communication with your horse takes time."

Remy pondered over Mazie's words. "Hmm, I like that. I will try to become 'one-with' horses. Then added, "Will you teach me how to ride horses and to become 'one-with'"?

Mazie hugged Remy, "Yes, I would love to."

Off in the distance, they could hear wolfs howling. Remy became excited and said, "Listen Mazie, there are wolfs in the forest."

"Yes… Yes… I can hear him." Mazie then told Remy a story. "A long time ago, the Spirt-Moon's reflection danced upon the waters. Spirt-Moon soon met the Spirit of the Wolf, and they danced together on the water's shoreline. Oh, how they enjoyed their dances together. One night, Spirit-Moon said it was her time to return to the heavens, and with one last dance, they embraced, and she was gone. And you know what? To this very day, all wolves cry to the moon in hopes that they may dance together."

Mazie then howled like a wolf. And instantly, Remy joined in howling.

# Chapter 19

Later that day, Mazie and Walter were out front of the veterinarian's hospital checking out a horse that had gone lame. Walter was swooshing a fly that kept buzzing his face. He laughed and asked Mazie, "You know what this is?" He asked while he swatted away a fly.

"What's that Sir?"

"When you brush away a fly. That's our Australian salute." Mazie looked into his eyes and laughed. She sure enjoyed his humor, goofy jokes, and how he could make her smile.

Briefly, their eyes locked together and they both beamed.

Mazie pointed over toward the bombed-out homestead of the Chateau Beau Vignoble. "Major Thompson, Sir, look over there. Hercules has escaped the corral again."

Walter looked over at what was left of the old house. "Crikey! He certainly is the escape artist, isn't he?" Laughingly, he spewed out, isn't this the fourth time this week he has escaped? Grab a halter, and let's go that catch that bloody bogan."

Mazie grabbed a halter, and they walked over into the old fenced-in flower garden.

"This garden is so sad to see; this must have been a beautiful flower garden before the war."

"Mmm, defo."

Hercules was in the far corner of the yard foraging without a care. Upon further investigation, it appeared that his hoof was caught in a hole, and he could not move. Mazie and Walter walked toward him. "Be careful Lieutenant, it looks like Hercules is standing on something."

The two bent down cautiously, and lifted, and brushed away debris holding Hercules's hoof. Mazie freed up his hoof, and the two led him to a tree in the garden where he was tethered.

Both returned to where Hercules had been stuck. "What the bloody hell is under this rubbish?"

Again, they sank to their knees and began removing debris, branches, and rocks.

"It looks like an old cellar door."

"Defo, ya right" Walter looked at Mazie, "Let's have a look."

After clearing off the cellar door and opening it, Mazie and Walter went down ten dust-covered steps, into the musty, drafty cellar. "Ace, would you look at this?" Still surprised he added, "Well if this is as unexpected as gunplay in a bible class."

Excited, Mazie replied, "I don't think anyone knows this wine cellar has survived the bombing."

Walter laughed heartily, "Look at all the bottles of Champagne!"

"This is so wonderful," Mazie said in awe. There must be dozens of bottles down here." Pointing toward the far end of the cellar, "Look, you can see where the end of the house and cellar was bombed. But, this portion of the cellar is unharmed."

Mazie remarked in awe. "I'll bet this was a grand house in its day. It is such a shame that it's been destroyed by the war." She ran her fingers over some wine bottles and wrote her name in the dust on a nearby small table. "It reminds me of a book I read by the author Charlotte Brontë, Jane Ayre, and the Moor Manor. Gosh! This is amazing!"

Walter pulled one of the bottles from the wine rack and read the label. "Chateau Beau Vignoble Champagne 1910." Playfully he added, "Ace year, shall we try a sip?"

Mazie's eyes widened, "I have never had Champagne before. But we have no glasses to drink it from."

"Not a problem." Walter wiped off the bottle with his handkerchief, then skillfully pooped the cork. Champagne spewed out of the bottle. Laughing, he poured a little of it on the ground and handed the bottle to Mazie. "Mademoiselle, here is to your first drink of heaven."

Mazie took a polite swig from the bottle. Her eyes widened, "It is so bubbly." Then exclaimed excitingly, "It tastes wonderful."

Walter took a drink of the Champagne. Mmm, Ace." Then continued after another swig. "And I'll take another drink because my sarcasm needs to stay hydrated."

They dusted off an old wooden lawn ottoman near the bombed-out part of the cellar moved it toward the door, and sat together drinking their found treasure. There was only joy in their eyes, smiles on their faces, and no present effects of the war haunting them. Time went on, and they shared their stories.

Walter chatted about Australia. And Mazie spoke about New Mexico. The two talked until they were no longer Major and Lieutenant in the horrific war but rather happy and peaceful friends.

Walter's broad smile revealed his white teeth in the dim light. Her heart responded to his warm smile. She couldn't help but look into his eyes to find an answer to her sudden adoration and admiration. The sheer power of him made her flutter. As their eyes met the attraction was too intense. It was a natural spontaneous response as he placed a gentle kiss tenderly on her lips. That simple kiss only demanded another. He drew her to him and kissed her again. His lips brushed back and forth across hers, nudging, pulling, and pressing open a pathway for his tongue to enter. Moist heat, silken-smooth, on a new swirl of sensations... Mazie forgot to breathe.

She opened her eyes, only to find him in return. His brows gathered while a sheer smile touched his lips. It was a kiss like nothing she had ever experienced or even dreamed of experiencing. She drew in a deep breath, but the wonderment overcame her, and she could not express her thoughts of awe.

Without hesitation, Walter's hand promptly found the back of her head and drew her closer to him. Then he kissed her with more eros than he had ever experienced. He could feel the thunder of her heartbeat, again, he kissed her tenderly. Then the kiss grew to one of ravishment, their tongues sensuously thrusting and exploring. Both withdrew, breathless and stunned by the tantalizing desires they felt. In ending the kiss, both sighed in amazement.

Mazie felt a raw energy about him that was undeniable, an electric current that drew her to him and that she found new and exciting.

Walter and Mazie bonded instinctively with the contour of each other's bodies, becoming closer and closer, molding in coexistence. Every kiss increased with a surge of tantalizing sensation. Mazie could smell him; it was a stimulating smell of maleness, affable, salty, and enigmatic. She could feel the power of his masculinity and basked comfortably in the combined energies generated by their closeness. Her attraction to Walter made her aflutter.

This gentle, alluring woman mesmerized Walter. She seemed embellished with a zeal and deep understanding of life, complete of earthliness and bewitching. She felt so right.

Trying to sober her intoxicatingly euphoric daze, Mazie said by way of conversation, "This cellar that we have found is quite the treasure. It is magical, and your kisses are also magical."

He playfully laughed. Pulling Mazie closer as if to protect her. "Ace! Yes, that was a delightful Pash." Laughing at himself, he added, Oh! A "pash" is Aussie, for a passionate kiss."

Mazie teasingly said, "Well, I certainly enjoyed that pash."

"How do you say kiss in your native language?" Walter asked with a big smile.

She answered in a dulcet tone, "In Mimbres, a kiss is a Kye."

"Miss Mazie, could I have another kye?"

Mazie leaned near him and gave him a heavenly kiss."

A delighted "Mmm!" Was his only response.

With a warm, sexy smile, he replied, "Mazie, you sure do make my heart sing."

Mazie was enjoying the moment and smiled.

Walter bent down and kissed her lightly on her forehead, and could smell the freshness of her sweet fragrant scent of femininity. It touched his senses like an intense aphrodisiac. "Mmm! Ace!" He said to himself quietly.

A tipsy, giddy rush rose up in Mazie quickly, and for the first time, she felt truly comfortable with a man.

Walter's quick wit fell short of supply, for he found no words to express other than, Bonzer!" And "Ta!"

They stayed embraced in each other arms for several minutes. However, they knew they had to get back to work.

Walter didn't want their time together to end, and he said he felt very awkward and apprehensive. "I would be honored if you would join me for dinner in the Mess-Tent tonight?"

Elated for the invitation, Mazie teased, "Only if you answer one quick question first?"

Puzzled he replied, "Yes, of course."

"Well then, Major, are you always this much of a gentleman?" Sighing, she said, "I've never met a man like you before." She offered a moderate giggle and shook her head in disbelief.

Returning with one of his homespun smiles, he slightly bowed, "Crikey! "Defo, I am."

She hated putting herself in with that shallow group who cared only for looks, and yet, she knew that her attraction to him was more powerful than his looks alone. Feeling good was easy when she was with him.

"Mazie, maybe we can escape to this cellar again soon." Giving her a light sweet kiss, he added, "But we must keep this hidden treasure a secret."

And they laughed at their agreement to keep the wine cellar a secret.

* * *

They managed to keep their interest for each other on professional level when around others. However, they did manage to sneak in many hugs, kisses, and endless flirting.

# Chapter 20

Several months had passed since Remy was brought to Fort Champagne and became the fort's child. Everyone enjoyed helping him, playing with him, and teaching him. Mazie and Remy had been training and exercising the horses. The arrival of the American tanks replaced the inconceivable battle tactics of charging into battle on horseback and instantaneously being slaughtered by machine guns. Although the war campaigns had moved away from using horses in combat, horses and mules were still an integral part of operations.

There were countless reports of bravery with men and women from all cultures and ethnic groups, and there were many who never received the mention nor honor they deserved during The Great War. Although it was very much a man's world or war, there were few American Women soldiers, and it was unthinkable for women to fight alongside men. Yet by the end of war, two hundred thousand women were in uniform. American women in the war were primarily cooks, ambulance drivers, and translators. Many served in operations, communications, and office support, and there was extraordinary support in the medical field from nurses in every capacity. The supporting American women back in the States was ranching, farming, transportation, and munitions work. Worldwide, over two million women took on jobs previously filled by men.

Rarely mentioned nor honored were the Harlem Hell Fighters, one of the few African-American units that saw the front lines. Although their deserved mention was noted for their extraordinary acts of heroism, the African-American soldiers did receive the French Croix de Guerre, a medal awarded to soldiers from Allied countries for bravery in combat. However, in the U.S., their deeds were largely ignored. There were more than two hundred thousand African Americans who served in the Great War, but only about eleven percent of them were in combat forces. The rest were in labor units, loading cargo, building roads, and digging ditches. They served in the segregated divisions of the 92nd and 93rd and trained separately from the other Amy units.

Also, during the Great War, thirteen thousand Native American soldiers served in the U.S. military, and tens of thousands of Native Americans supported the war at home by working in war industries and assisting in war relief efforts. American Indian soldiers were praised for their bravery at the front. Still the stereotypes about Native Americans as natural "warriors" led to dangerous combat assignments that resulted in higher casualty rates than those for white soldiers.

American Indians volunteered to serve despite a long history of discrimination against indigenous people and their traditional culture. Native Americans weren't even recognized as U.S. citizens. Shamefully, few Native American warriors who fought in the War were honored for their unique tactics and involvement.

* * *

Lieutenant-Colonel William J. Morrissey of the 142nd Infantry, 36th Division, stopped in Fort Champagne on their way to their assigned location. It was a blustery afternoon when a small troop came marching through and stopped to rest at Fort Champagne. For Mazie, it was awe-inspiring to discover the troops were all Native American.

As the Native American troops were resting, Mazie and Remy visited them.

Remy was so excited, "Look, Mazie, these soldiers are Indians like you."

With pride, Mazie greeted the troops. "Welcome to Fort Champagne, I trust your travels have been good?"

Using his native Apache language, one of the men in the group called out to Mazie. "What is a Native Woman doing in the Army?"

Astonished to hear her own native tongue, she called out. "How did you know I was Mimbres." Mazie knew that there were over a thousand languages for American indigenous people.

A short husky man with a leathered face, large wet eyes the color of black obsidian came over to her and shook her hand and said in English. "I didn't know; I was just hoping and guessing. But I am happy to know you are of my people."

Remy stood next to her with his mouth open, gaping in awe. And it seemed everyone at the Fort stopped to watch.

"Da'anzho!" She greeted him. Where are you from my brother?"

He answered, "Mescalero, New Mexico. I am known as George Waquie." Noticing her rank by the bars on her uniform, he then asked her. "Lieutenant, where are you from, my sister?"

Mazie's heart was singing with pride. "I am of the Mimbres Tribe, from Mimbres, New Mexico." Smiling, she told him, "My name is Mazie Atencio, but my people called me Horse Girl." She then called out to all who could hear her. "Welcome, all my brothers." In unison, they returned a cheer of gratitude. Many came to shake her hand. Soon, several of the personnel from Fort Champagne came to greet them, including Walter.

"Sergeant George Waquie, I would like to introduce you to Major Walter Thompson of the Australian 9th Light Horse Regiment." Adding, "Major Thompson is Fort Champagne's veterinarian." Mazie was proud to introduce Walter to her native brother, George.

"Good to meet you, Mate." The two met eye to eye and shook hands. "Sergeant Waquie, do you and your men care to join us in our mess tent for lunch."

"Yes, Captain Thompson, we would like that."

Mazie quickly spoke to Remy, "Remy, run and tell Big-Bean that we have several guests joining us for lunch."

Excited, Remy ran off to the mess tent.

Mazie, Walter, Remy, and George sat together at a table. Walter offered his warm and wonderful smile along with his friendly energy. "In Australia, we have Native Aboriginals, of whom I am proud to claim that I grew up with. I honor and cherish their way of life, the lessons they taught me hunting, and horsemanship, and their spiritual understanding. I am surprised to see that your units' troops are mostly Native Americans."

"Yes, brother, most American Indian soldiers have been integrated into divisions of the American Expeditionary Force, but a few units, such as our Company E of the 36th Division, we are entirely Native American." Pointing to the patch on his shoulder, he said, "This insignia is an original design for the 36th Division; it features a blue arrowhead to represent Oklahoma Indians." He turned to

Mazie and said a few words to her in their native language, then continued. "Most of our Native American troops are used as scouts, snipers, and code-talkers." George's stern military demeanor quickly changed, and he laughed, "However, on the front lines, we have been assigned to be scouting enemy snipers. Those damn blood-thirsty military commanders hide behind their desks to observe the war, believing that we would be comfortable in that role. Some commanders see our group as primed for battle, on the idea that we are naturally warrior-like."

George turned to young Remy, ran his hand through Remy's hair, messing it up, then playfully teased. "How! Young white man!"

This brought laughter to everyone.

Giggling, Remy returned, "How! Chief George."

Then George changed back to a more candid, severe tone, "Their racist beliefs and ideas mean there is an unusually high population of American Indians being sent into dangerous situations compared to the average soldier in the Army."

The raw power of his words gave Mazie the chills.

Fort Champagnes British Commander, Lieutenant Colonel Nicolas Jernigan came busting into the mess hall and gallantly announced, "What's going on here? This isn't no pow-wow! Everyone, back to work."

Expressionless, George stood slowly and proudly, all the while staring at Commander Jernigan. Looking into the Commander's eyes, George looked as if he felt sorry for him for being the dumb-ass that he was portraying himself to be.

Their stay at Fort Champagne was brief as the infantry was heading to the front lines only thirty miles away near the town of Cambrai in northeast France. Two days following, George and his company entered into a brutal armed conflict. Shamefully, all wars throughout history are marked as revolting acts of mankind; however, the battle in the countryside of Cambrai that day was gruesome beyond description.

Russia had just signed an armistice with Germany, thus provoking the Germans to rage further into France. There had already been three years of endless war efforts with Germans dying by the thousands, yet they didn't seem to be depleted, let alone exhausted.

The town and the surrounding countryside of Cambrai received the most brutal artillery barrage of the war; some one thousand five hundred rounds were fired that night, six rounds a minute ragging on for more minutes than anyone could bear to count. Sometimes, the combined troops and allies put out so much firepower toward the Germans that the allies couldn't tell whether any of the German artillery was coming back on them. The noise was deafening; it filled their ears and heads until they thought they had lost hearing. And the smell and stench of cordite acid hung in the air, burning their nostrils and lungs and turning their stomachs.

American troops had rows and rows of tanks coming… And the might of hundreds of ally soldiers from France, Australia, India, Britain, and America, treading in with a frighteningly powerful force… It was easy for George and his men to tell where their perimeter was that night by hearing and seeing the sky light up from gunfire. They patrolled in the dark while the ghostly enemy attackers ran within battle fringes in the woods. They were ready to die right there rather than fail. There was absolutely no regard for human life or any living thing.

Some of the American Marines in a nearby war zone joked that the Native American 36th Division was merely bait. But on this night, the Native American troops held their own and raged into battle with absolute precision and control. As the gunfire came toward them in extreme intensity, they could no more than blink or spit. It was balls and bowels turning over together, their senses working like strobes, their adrenaline spiking every essence of their being. It became an intense rush of focus, a yo-yo of instincts reaching out from calm, followed by a spring of warped pleasurable excitement that was infused with dread. It was that dread that would be known by every warrior who ever lived, unutterable in its speeding brilliance, touching all the edges and then passing as though it had all been controlled from outside by a demon.

A Comanche from Oklahoma, Private Calvin Atchavit was among George's company; he fought with the spirit of a true warrior. Archivist's left arm had been severely wounded. Fighting with only one arm, his adrenaline rush distracted his rage of pain, allowing him to maintain superior marksmanship and precision aim in shooting and killing the enemy. Equally impressive was that Atchavit captured four prisoners.

Desperate to help the injured troops, everyone from Front Champagne was instantly on alert and assigned to aid the fallen soldiers. Most of their assigned duties were to drive ambulances to recover the hundreds of fallen men from the battle of Cambrai. Walter and his unit rushed to give medical help to the fallen. There hadn't been enough ambulances to recover all needing aid, so Mazie gathered nearby lumber and made travois to be pulled by the Fort Champagne's mules. Men were loaded up on the travois and hauled back to the Fort.

Wanting to help, Mazie had ridden Hercules to the Cambrai battle site, pulling a travois behind her. She was flagged down by Sergeant George Waquie. One of his men, Private Atchavit, was in immediate need of medical treatment. When she came to Archivist's aid, her breath was sent down into her boots from the shocking sight of his left arm hanging merely from his body's muscle and sinew strands. She quickly took off her undershirt and belt. She wrapped his arm to his chest and tightened her belt around his upper torso, trying to keep his arm from falling off. "Hang in there brother, I'll get you to the medical tent as soon as I can." With cold white lips, Atchavit offered her a survivor's smile, then spoke to her in his native language. Even though she couldn't understand his tribal dialect, she could feel his energy of gratitude.

It seemed like dragging the travois back to the fort took hours. All the while, Archivist's face remained utterly expressionless. When they finally got back to the fort, and as they were taking Atchavit into the medical tent, he told Mazie. "Thank you, my sister, for helping me. I thanked God for sending me such a beautiful warrior to help me." It took all that she had not to tear up.

* * *

After the Cambrai battle, George Waquie slowly staggered around the now quiet combat zone; he was so weary and empty that he only wanted to sit and think about being alive, yet he stumbled around checking on his Indian brothers from Company E, 36th Division. His hearing was faint, and his ears rang so loud that he was having trouble thinking. When he finally got to rest, his adrenaline hangover took hold of him, and he curled up in a ball and slept for fifteen hours straight. When he awoke, George didn't want to recall any confrontation. Yet even though the ground action had been over for hours, he still had a compulsive replay. The battle details remained obscure to him for a long time until his memory took shape and reality finally revealed itself.

# Chapter 21

After weeks of privately flirting with each other, Walter, and Mazie agreed to sneak down to the champagne cellar to meet. They both had gales of laughter as they made their way to their secret hiding place.

"Mazie, I brought down to the cellar some fresh straw and blankets. "Oh! And I brought us some glasses to drink our Champagne out of." Then he asked her, "Which bottle of Champagne should we experience?"

"Hmmm! How about this one with the pretty flowery label?"

"Ace! Fine choice you have made my Lady." He said with a French accent. He opened the bottle, and poured it into their glasses, and handed Mazie a glass. "Cheers!"

Mazie felt comfortable and uninhibited and enjoyed the spontaneity, and chimed in. "Cheers!" Laughing, she added, "Here is to this marvelous cellar that we can sneak off to."

"Ace!  Cheers to this cellar."

Not wanting to relive the horrors of last week's battle, they talked about the Fort, and Remy, and slowly drank their Champagne.

They kissed until their blissful kisses soon grew into ravishment and desire.

Walter started to unbutton Mazie's uniform shirt and sweetly asked, "Are you okay with this?"

Mazie nodded and smiled, "Yes!" She felt very comfortable.

Walter finished unbuttoning Mazie's shirt and slipped her jacket and shirt off her. Then, with genuine concern, Walter said. "Let's keep your jacket on you, I don't want you to get cool."

Mazie returned the gesture and unbuttoned Walter's uniform shirt. Removing his shirt only affirmed his broad shoulders and revealed his muscular chest. She then realized she was actually with a man, who for the first time in her life, seemed to fulfill every letter of her desire. Though their clothing prevented any further intimate contact, the ample swell of manhood beneath his pants gave Mazie bold evidence of his masculinity.

She wasn't worried about hiding her flushed cheeks and didn't question her actions. This moment seems so natural to her. With a feeling of laissez-faire, she said. "Cheers! Again."

Walter moved closer to her and said with a smile so caring and warm it could have melted the snow that was falling outside, "Mazie, you are the most enchanting woman I have ever met." He marveled at this ravishing woman who had an unexplainable spark of life. She oozed freedom and awareness. She belonged to nobody other than herself, yet she was able to generously give of herself to everyone she met. She was pure magic. Captivated, he thought to himself, she is so sensuous. She was the personification of sensuality. In the dim light of the cellar, her coffee-brown eyes looked up to him with assurance as if she had an answer to his every question.

She then responded with a smile so pure that Walter's heart skipped a beat. She said in a faint whisper, "Kiss me." Which led them into a kiss that they both felt enthralled in an inescapable cocoon of desire.

Walter's mind overtook all human reasoning, his male animal instincts needed to make love to her. He kissed her slowly and tantalizingly, with increased anticipating passion. They molded together naturally and sank steadily onto the blanket-covered straw-bed floor. Their kiss grew to sexual intensity, and their desire increased as he slowly nibbled and kissed her throat, working down to the warm space between her supple breasts. He paused and looked into her eyes checking to see if she wanted him to go on. Mazie kissed him as if agreeing she wanted more and pushed away any of her jacket that hid her breasts. Her explosion of desire overtook him at the sight of her beautiful bare breast. As his hands explored, nimbly, yet gently, rolling her nipples between his fingers. Mazie's lustful gasps lead to a whirlwind of intensity and wild passion. Walter complimented this by skillfully sucking on her breasts.

In the desperation of sexual hunger, they quickly, frantically removed their pants and underclothing. Walter gently pulled her on top of him. As her small, exquisite body lay on top of his, she could feel his firm desire. Through passionate kisses, their bodies bonded together. Rapturous waves of pleasure began to roll through her loins as his hand began stroking the curling of the soft down between her legs, then teasing the lovely moist lips of her womanhood. She quietly whispered her sweet moans of pleasure. Suddenly, as if overtaken by an entity named passion, he rolled over on top of her. Walter intensified his kiss, then gently drove in the zeppelin of his manhood, penetrating her by exquisitely gradual degrees until she begged him to fill her completely. It was as if the Goddess of passion and desire had taken over and was choreographing their every move.

Their partnership continued in a tet-a-tete, like a slow sexual dance. Succumbed from desire, she gasped, "Yes! Yes, I need you." Her arms locked around his strong neck, and her slender legs tightened around him as he penetrated more profoundly, and forcefully. He explored every inch of her femininity, eventually together forming an exquisite ongoing rhythm, unending until their passion was used up. Then, they laid there holding each other in bliss, basking in the glow and feeling as if they were entwined and levitating. Time became irrelevant.

# Chapter 22

It was a foul weather day, and the gloominess of it sent Mazie, Adeline, and Remy sitting around in the dining hall. Big Bean was telling them a story while Mazie and Adeline were playing cards and Remy was tinkering on the piano. Walter came in from the rain. He was shaking off the wetness and adjusting his clothing when Adeline asked him, "Is it raining?"

Walter laughed and said, "No, I just went for a walk-in with my pet goldfish." The room was filled with laughter from Walter's cheeky answer. Walter sat next to Remy and gave him a hug.

They were busy with their card game when two British officers came in abruptly and arrogantly burst into the mess hall. Everyone in the room stood at attention. American soldiers always showed their respect of rank with British officers. However, British soldiers never returned the same respect when it came to American officers. It was Fort Champagnes British Lieutenant Colonel Nicolas

Jernigan and another British Colonel, Warrick Nithercott. Standing at attention, Jernigan theocratically announced, "Colonel Warrick Nithercott and I are here concerning this young boy who is being kept here at Fort Champagne, and that you all have made a pet of. I know of your shenanigans in feeding, housing, and caring for this young scoundrel." Jernigan then pointed at Remy, "Colonel Nithercott this the young boy who we are talking about?"

Walter walked toward them. "With all due respect…"

Without allowing Walter to finish his sentence, Colonel Nithercott, immediately interrupted, "You cannot play wet nurse to a local boy. I will be taking this lad to the Saint Mary's Orphanage in Paris." He spoke precipitately and arrogantly and commanded his respect.

Confusion and concern instantly swept over everyone at the table, and everyone sprang to the defense of Remy and began questioning Colonel Nithercott's announcement.

Remy was in shock and started crying. "No, Walter, you told me I would not have to go to an or-fig-nage … No…" Pleading, he continued, "Mazie, please don't let him take me…"

There was a growing outcry of voices. Walter stepped even closer to Colonel Nithercott. "Sir, I heed your warning. And I request that you give me time to find a home for Remy."

Remy gave everyone a fearful, searching glance, his eyes flooded with tears and disbelief, and his face was frantically alarmed.

Ludicrously open and bragging with a sordid face, Colonel Jernigan beamed and said, "Major Thompson and Lieutenant Atencio, I have been warning you for months that you need to find care for this boy." He was proud of himself, for he was certain he had called the situation correctly.

Mazie cried, "Please sir… We need a few days to find Remy a safe home. We promised Remy that we would not put him in an orphanage…"

Colonel Nithercott boldly interrupted her sentence, "Lieutenant, this is wartime. I could give a rats-ass what you promised the boy. He will be removed from Fort Champagne immediately and taken directly to Saint Mary's Home.

Remy ran over to Mazie and wrapped his arms around her waist with a frightfully strong grasp; tears flooded his eyes as he pleaded, "No, Mazie. Don't let them take me."

Commander Lieutenant Colonel Jernigan rushed over to Mazie and tried to pry the boy away from Mazie.

Mazie brazenly screamed at Colonel Jernigan, "Damn it, Nick, you bastard. At least give me a few minutes to talk to Remy."

Colonel Jernigan was scared by her reaction. He had never seen this side of Mazie and took warning. "You have five minutes, Lieutenant."

Mazie was overwhelmed and flooded with fear. She didn't know what to say… What could she do to stop this? Mazie led Remy away from Colonel Jernigan. She knelt next to him and hugged him. "Shh, shh, shh… My sweet Remy" She gently rocked him back and forth until he calmed down enough for her to continue, "Shh, I need you to be a strong little man and listen to what I have to say… Can you do that? Where is my strong man?"

Remy wiped his nose on this sleeve, trembling, and he nodded. "Yes… I am strong."

She offered him a brave smile. "Strong like Hercules?"

He offered a weak laugh, "Yes… Strong like Hercules."

She was so unnerved; she couldn't think of anything positive to say to Remy. She was having trouble speaking. And she knew she needed to sound brave for Remy. "Remy, my dear little man… hmm… I…" Her eyes tearing up.

Walter could see she was having trouble and rushed over to the two of them and joined in on their hug. "Hey there, little Mate, you are the strongest little man I've ever met. You will be fine. Mazie and I will come to visit you and look after you."

Mazie's bravery finally kicked in. She settled her mind and drew strength from her soul. Mazie then took Remy's hand and put it on her heart, then took her hand and placed it on his heart. "In my heart, you are deeply ingrained. You make everything in this unsettled world a little more wonderful. I need you to know how much you matter to me, Walter, and to all of us here."

Everyone in the room nodded and said, "That's right."

Clearing her throat, she continued. "Remy, I will do all I can to keep in touch with you and visit you as often as I possible. But right now, I need you to be strong." Pausing, she continued, "It is undeniable that you will continue to make a difference in the world with whomever you are with or wherever you are. Just think how amazing it is that our God has created wondrous oceans, marvelous mountains, and miraculous sky filled with endless stars and galaxies. And Remy, God has also made someone as remarkable as you. You, my sweet Remy, are an extraordinary young man. Hold your head high because you are amazing."

Tearfully, Remy nodded his approval and gave Mazie a big strong hug, then turned to Walter and gave him a big hug.

Colonel Nithercott interrupted. Does anyone know this boy's surname?

Remy answered proudly, "My last name is Agen. I am Remy Agen."

As if he was speaking from a regulation book, Colonel Nithercott pompously said, "The British Army will be sure that Master Remy Agen is properly placed in the care of Saint Mary's Orphanage in Paris."

Colonel Jernigan then stood behind Remy and led him toward the door.

Colonel Nithercott patted Jernigan on the back and said, "Stupendously done, Lieutenant Colonel Jernigan, I am quite surrencified."

There wasn't a dried eye in the room as Lieutenant Colonel Jernigan and Colonel Nithercott led Remy out the door and loaded him in the British Rolls-Royce Armored car.

Everyone is the dining hall was stunned. Fumbling his words Big Bean said, "That Colonel Jernigan is a mean bugger. He is mean enough to steal the coins off a dead man's eyes." Shaking his head in disbelief.

Mazie didn't care who was watching, and she rushed to Walter arms. Sobbing, "Oh my hell, I can't believe this has happened." Walter gently wiped the tears from her cheeks.

Shaking her head, she continued, "I was at a loss for words, I didn't know what to say to Remy… I feel so guilty… We promised Remy we would not send him to an orphanage." Her guilt made her feel like a thousand spiders were crawling over her.

Water held her tight and kissed her forehead.

Even though almost everyone had suspected that there was affection between them, the only person in the room who knew there was a spark between them was Adeline.

Surprised by the affection that Water and Mazie openly showed toward each other, Big-Bean's mouth dropped open; he took off his cook's hat, scratched his head, and said, "Well, I'll be damn!"

With a weak smile, Water looked over at him and replied, "Most of us are."

Wanting to calm her mind by keeping herself busy, Mazie decided to return to working with the horses. She was brushing one of the mules when she heard a man yelling from one of the nearby stables. As she hurried over to see what the commotion was about, she witnessed a British soldier shouting at a buckskin mare. "What the fuck is wrong with you? You old nag." Why won't you move? The private then punched the Mare in the face. The Mare let out a winching sound of pain.

"This day couldn't get much worse," Mazie hurried to the mare and noticed the mare was in labor. Mazie marched up to the Private, kicking him with all her might; she kicked him in the balls. "What the hell are you doing? Can't you see this mare is in labor?" The private let out a scream and immediately crumbled to the ground in agony. Several nearby soldiers rushed to see what the racket was about.

Mazie was ashamed that she reacted that way, but she had built up a tremendous amount of anger, and that poor guy just received the brunt of it. Within seconds, many more people, including Walter, came to see what the commotion was about.

Walter stepped in to aid the mare in labor. Mazie assisted. After several minutes the foal was born. Witnessing the birth of the beautiful foal calmed her anger and made her realize, yes it seemed the world was upside down, but there are still a lot of God's miracles to witness.

* * *

The war was going well now that American troops were in place on the Eastern front of France. The combined efforts of the allies and the one million US troops created a dynamic war power. The power of the forces sustained success and defeat against the Germans and pushed the Germans back.

# Chapter 23

Two weeks after Remy was taken from the Fort, Mazie and Walter made a trip to Saint Mary's Orphanage which is located on the eastern outskirts of Paris. They entered the plain and drab yet squeaky clean front room parlor and were told to wait there. A tall, thin nun came in with Remy. Both Mazie and Walter stood to greet him. Remy was so excited to see them that he started to run over to them, only to have the nun pull him back and hold him by his shirt. She gave him a severe scolding. "No! Master Remy, we do not run in the orphanage."

"Yes, Sister Margaret." Remy began to tear up and slowly made his way over to a chair near Walter and Mazie.

Then Sister Margaret hissed at Remy, Walter, and Mazie, "You are allowed a thirty-minute visit. When your thirty minutes are up, I will return to retrieve Master Remy. Then, Master Remy you are to report back to the kitchen to finish your chores." She stared sternly at Mazie, then closed the door to the parlor.

Remy went running into their arms. Mazie kissed his little cheeks over and over. The three embraced in a beautiful-loving hug for several minutes.

How are you, little Mate? Walter ruffed up Remy's hair.

"Are you here to take me back to the Fort?"

It took Mazie all she could do not to cry when she heard his question. "No, we are sorry Remy we cannot take you back with us; we only came to visit."

Tearing up Remy questioned, "Okay. But someday soon you will take me with you?"

Both Mazie and Walter said, "Yes, we will."

Walter added, "Yes! Defo, hopefully soon when the bloody war is over."

Mazie tried to lighten the mood. "So, how are you, my little man? What do you do all day? Are you learning a lot in school?"

"Yeah, well, my English is getting better. The nuns here are really strict. I get punished a lot because of my big mouth. But I am learning to play the piano. I love the piano."

Walter teased Remy, "Hey Little Mate, what is invisible and smells like carrots?"

"I do not know."

Walter laughed out the answer, "Bunny farts!"

Remy laughed so hard he had tears in his eyes. Golly, how he loved and adored and missed Walter and Mazie.

"Remy, I decided I am going to give you a broken drum for your birthday."

"A broken drum? Why would you give a broken drum?"

Walter chuckled, "Because you can't beat it."

The three sat and chatted for several minutes when Mazie noticed seven or eight children peeking into the windows. Mazie asked Remy, "Are these your friends?"

Remy laughed and went to the window and opened it. "Yeah, I told them all about you being an Indian, and they didn't believe me. So, I guess they came to see for themselves." Remy opened the widow and said proudly to the children outside, "See, I didn't make this up. She really is an Indian from the United States of America."

Mazie laughed, went to the window, and said, "Hello, boys and girls."

The children all said hello and gleamed with delight from meeting Mazie. Some children started chanting and howling and ran around in circles, patting their mouths and making war cries.

Mazie laughed and mimicked the children's war cries and gestures.

Suddenly, an older nun came charging into the parlor waving a stick. "You heathen-devil! Stop that evil racket."

Maize and Walter thought the nun was going to strike them with her stick. Suddenly, two more nuns came rushing in.

Remy started to cry. Mazie was in shock over the incident. Walter quickly stepped in front of Mazie and Remy to protect them. "Hold on there, Sister…"

"Hold on… You dare correct me." Turning briefly to the other two Sisters, she barked out orders. "Sister Margaret and Sister Agnes, take Master Remy to his room immediately." The nuns rushed over to Remy and carried him out as he was crying, kicking, and screaming.

Walter stood determined and noble. "Where is your shame, Sister? You cannot bully us like you do your orphan children. Stop this nonsense."

"Nonsense? This is not… Ba!" She pointed her finger at Mazie, and continued, "Young man take this Indian-heathen and leave Saint Mary's now… And never return." She puffed up her chest and forced them out the front door while she continually shook her bony figure at them the entire way. She slammed the front door of the orphanage, and Walter and Mazie could hear her yelling and calling out orders. Now they could hear many of the children crying.

Trying to make light of the deplorable scene that they had just left, Walter joked. "Crikey! I feel like I just cracked my halo." Disgusted by the actions of the nuns, then added in a serious tone, "That is not a Christian house of God. The mental abuse of the children and the prejudice we just witnessed is appalling."

Mazie said calmly and gracefully, "None of us sit high enough to look down on anybody." Shaking her head, she added. "Oh my! Walter, we must find a way to get Remy out of there."

For a few miles, they rode in silence. Releasing a huge sigh, Mazie said, "I'd rather let my spirit fly free than be caged by the Catholic religion." With self-confidence, she added, "When hate is loud, love must be louder. Dear Lord, I pray for peace in the hearts of those sinister nuns. And peace for the children."

Walter was impressed by her reserve and was so proud of Mazie in the way that she held her head high and withstood prejudice. He looked over at her in admiration. How he adored her; she didn't let her wild beauty be tamed. She didn't allow her heart to be swayed by the opinions of others. She didn't allow her individuality to be trapped by a blizzard of prejudice or by trying to please the world. And Mazie wasn't about to be restricted by someone else's ignorance and fear. Ah! Yes, he thought, all this allowed Mazie's true beauty to be free.

Water and Mazie remained in a state of shock and sadness the entire way back to the Fort.

* * *

Unbeknownst to Walter and Mazie, the Reverend Mother was so revolted by the incident she had Remy transferred to another orphanage on the West Coast of Cardiff, England. And refused to let anyone know where he was sent to.

# Chapter 24

Walter and Mazie decided to use their R and R and head to the coast. The drive had become a labyrinth with interconnecting country roads branching out through the zenith of the seductive coastal byways. Mazie took in all the scenery. She was enjoying being away and out exploring the countryside. The motor carriage was just noisy enough that they couldn't carry on a conversation. Walter was enjoying the drive through the whimsical countryside he called out to Mazie, "This drive is like a carnival ride, and we didn't even need a ticket."

Mazie laughed and smiled.

The overhanging trees above them engulfed the road as they twisted and turned down an old dirt road, which lay just a quarter mile from the ocean. With one final bend, they turned off onto a sweet, secluded seaside little yellow cottage, or what the French called Villa, which was located south of the small village of Cayeux-sur-Mer.

Walter helped Mazie down from the motor carriage and guided her into the villa.

Mazie was in awe over the stunning view of the ocean below. The unspoiled nature and white sandy beaches below. "Look at this, Walter. I have never seen anything this beautiful." Excited she gave Walter a sweet little kiss. "Thank You for bringing me here." Silently, she looked around the refreshing landscape.

"Ya are welcome, my dear."

They walked into the villa holding hands.

The petite house whispered echoes from the past. It was a small one-room house with a bed, two wooden chairs, a small table, and a gorgeous stone fireplace. Next to the bed, was an enclave to the bathroom, which had a tiny sink squished in next to the toilet. The entire bathroom wall was small baseball-size smooth—river rocks skillfully tucked into white plaster. Mazie rubbed her hand over the rock wall, admiring its artwork and spectacular craftsmanship. The rock bathroom wall also served as a shower wall.

Walter and Mazie quickly found themselves wrapped together. Walter's hand swiftly lifted to the back of her head, drew her to him, and then he kissed her. Nudging, pressing, and then opening a pathway for his tongue to enter. Moist heat, silken-smooth, on a new swirl of sensations... Mazie was momentarily lost in the divine, enigmatic essence of their kiss.

Mazie opened her eyes only to find his eyes in return. Trying to cover the burst of passion and desire she was suddenly flooded with. She drew in a deep breath and flamboyantly exclaimed, "What a wonderful kiss." Then, with a sweet, sincere voice, "Thank You, I have never been kissed like that."

Walter became embarrassed that he had so quickly taken advantage of her kiss. He laughed, "Oh! Ah...Ya... let me bring our luggage in." Trying to regain his composure, "Wait until ya see the basket of tucker, ya friend Adeline packed for us."

After Walter had brought in their belongings, he started futzing with the wood in the fireplace. "I am going to build ya a small fire to take the chill off." Walter removed his jacket and neckerchief, tossed them along with his hat into a chair, and then rolled up his sleeves, instinctively making himself more comfortable with his surroundings.

After settling in, Walter sat and watched Mazie, who was staring into the fire and joyfully examining the cozy little one-room house, looking at the bed that also served as a couch. The tiny cabin was screaming with authentic French country charm.

Walter was certain he had called the situation correctly, Mazie had an aura of lethal feminism, and she was as profoundly exotic, seductive, and alluring.

They stood together, watching the flames dance in the fire with their fingers entangled together. Mazie laid her head on Walter's chest, and she listened to his heartbeat; it made her feel safe, like nothing wrong could ever happen. She looked up into his eyes and was drawn to a loving kiss. The sweetness of their kiss soon kindled into stormy desire. A simple kiss grew to a passionate kiss; as time became immemorial, they slowly melted harmoniously onto the floor. Though her clothing prevented any intimate contact, she was very aware of his needs. He continued to kiss her, taking care to slowly arouse her senses, until their kiss stormed into what became a kiss of ravishment, their tongues sensuously thrusting, exploring. His hands moved into her hair. His fingers caressed her cheeks like the softest whisper, trailing and teasing her lips, circling her ears, skimming over her neck, causing her to shiver with delight. No part of her escaped his caressing, her arms, shoulders, hands, and breasts, all without removing their clothes, slowly as if he wanted to braille every inch of this lovely being forever into his memory.

Walter asked her with genuine gentlemanly concern, "Mazie, are ya okay with us making love?"

She answered quickly, "Hmph, I have never met a man I was so attracted to." She paused, not believing her erotic appetite, "Walter…" She looked into his smiling eyes. "Yes, I want to make love with you…" She wanted to touch him, to tease him, to trail her fingers over his firm body and explore what was unknown and savor his intoxicating maleness.

Water picked her off the floor and gently set her on the bed.

She reached up with her lips to meet his, then deepened her kiss, only to provoke and tantalize her growing needs. Breathless, "Walter…" Never finishing her sentence, suddenly caught up in a desiring kiss, as if his returned kiss answered her question. Beyond that, no words were spoken, only their echoed moans and deep sighs that whispered with the flickering flames of the fire.

Their passion ignited to a blaze. Walter became a noble beast, gracefully possessed in an erotic flight, a male animal who did nothing overtly to overpower. Yet his power was what she wanted at this moment.

Mazie sat up, bringing Walter up with her, all the while drawing his kiss.

She could smell his maleness, the slick, salty, steamy smell of worked-up pheromones. She began to unbutton his shirt, trailing her lips over his neck, savoring the salty taste of him, her hands fondled and stimulated his soft, muscular chest, gracefully laying back and continuing her exploration to his firm stomach, gently unfastening his pants, freeing his swelling male shaft. Oh, he felt so good to her, so different, so strong, and so intoxicating.

"Walter," she whispered breathlessly, "I need you to make love to me!" Silently, he answered his agreement by deepening his kiss. Again, he was bombarding her with tantalizing passion.

Her erotic appetite for him was overwhelming. Their sexual metronome ticking, repeating to the twin beat of the pounding rhythm of their hearts; gracefully, breathlessly, poetically, they removed each other's clothing, intensifying into a blaze as they wrapped their glistening naked bodies together.

The fire in her eyes entranced him. His lips tasted hers, then he gently nibbled on her ear, onto her neck, then downward, trailing his tongue to the soft ruby nipples of her small silky breasts, only to have her explode with wild desire. He awoke her inner Goddess. She moaned her approval as his hands continued to caress her lovely, lush body and taste the exhilarating nectar of her sweet flesh.

"Walter!" Gasping for air, she murmured softly,

breathlessly.

"Walter!... I need you now!" Calling out again with a voice that did not sound like her own.

Walter steadily climbed on top of Mazie and tenderly began caressing the moist, silky lips of her womanhood, preparing them for his sweltering lust. A rush of eroticism exploded in Mazie as Walter plunged the rod of his desire inside her slowly and teasingly, and her hips rose to meet his enveloping loins with a rush of passion. His strength for her was stunning. She loved the feel of him inside her. He glided in and out, forcefully, yet with exquisite care. Her arms closed tightly around him, and her hips rose to meet him. He pulled her into him, and she-onto him. The more he surged into her, the more he hungered to appease his craving for rapture. Their sexual momentum continued to intensify for an inexhaustible duration, plunging deeper and deeper with many bursts of unbelievable pulsating pleasure, finally ending... Concluding in the same ecstasy.

Time elapsed during their lovemaking, with only a few remaining glowing embers left in the fireplace. Yet Walter and Mazie continued to lie in bed in a dream-like sequence, imprinting the feel of each other, never once loosening their embrace. Mazie's legs trembled from their passion.

*   *   *

As the shadow crossed the time dial, slowly, they were returning once again to the real world, neither of them wanting to leave the unheeding zeal of their passion. They moved onto the porch and sat on the porch-step naked and wrapped together in a blanket. Looking out over the beach and ocean below, they exchanged small talk and stories of how it was at home. They exchanged sweet kisses and laughed about silly things no one else would have thought funny.

Walter remarked, "Sure is nice being here in the peaceful woop woop."

She laughed, then questioned? "What is woop woop?"

"Ya knows? It's the middle of nowhere, where there isn't a human to be seen. We are totally secluded." Adding, "And being away from the bloody war."

She let out a big sigh, "Yes, it truly is wonderful."

Walter then added, "It's aces being here with ya."

Amused by his Australian dialect. Again, she giggled, "Yes, it's aces."

* * *

Mazie took time out to thank God for this treasured ethereal moment. She relished the beauty of this natural world and its magnificent sights, the sounds of the waves, and the scents of the salty ocean breeze mixed with the sweet fragrance of wildflowers and the green shrubs that surrounded their Villa. She gave thanks for God's expressions of the divine.

Gracefully, she quoted scripture, "God saw everything that he had made, and indeed, it was very good."

Walter sighed, "Hmm, Genesis…"

In silence, they watch the sun extinguish into the ocean. Enjoying the ocean breeze, they continued sitting on the porch, eating bread, fruit, and cheese with a glass of Gare de Rouen red wine.

Mazie confessed, "I think I'm getting a taste for red wine and Champagne." Chuckling, "It is unquestionably good, or as you would say… Dinkum."

Trying to give her the full Aussie effect, Walter poured on the slang, "Ta Shelia that bronzer. Ya defo have learned words from my Straya."

Mazie laughed for a hearty length of time, then teased. "Ya, Walter, that's ace."

The full moon blazed from the eastern sky as they continued to sit together on the porch, wrapped in a blanket. A few clouds sailed by, covering the moon. Mazie scolded the cloud cover, "Go away, clouds. I want to see the moon."

Unwrapping himself from the blanket, Walter stood up, lifted his naked ass up toward the moon, and called out laughing, "See here, Mister Moon, this is how ya do it."

Mazie laid back on the porch floor and laughed. She pulled him down to her, and still laughing, she kissed him on the forehead. "You, Walter, are a funny man." Laughing her every other word, "How is it that you are still single?"

With a very serious look on his face, Walter answered. "Hmm, I am embarrassed to tell ya. Cause, I guess I learned my lesson and stopped chasing after women while I was in college. Ah…, Cause I mailed a letter and my picture to the Australian Lonely Heart Club, and they sent it back-Return to Sender."

# Chapter 25

The new dawn awoke, bringing the eastern morning's first light onto the ocean below. The water illuminated amid the austere beauty of the bright shimmering ocean... as if Mother Nature suddenly turned on a light. Truly this land was shaped and painted from the hands of the master sculptor... a master creator. Mazie stood on the porch of the le petite Maison-villa. Her thoughts filtered over the previous day she had spent with Walter. She knew that this was magic, this was spiritual; and this was true divinity, totally unabashedly and unashamed alchemy. This was so right.

Walter came and stood beside her.

In awe, Mazie proclaimed, "This is so...incredibly beautiful. No wonder you love the ocean."

Walter explained with tremendous pride, "Its beauty has a way of welcoming ya heart, as well as, settling ya mind."

Walter and Mazie walked to the nearby village of Cayeux-sur-Mer, and ate lunch at a quaint little café. Lightheartedly meandering through the shops, Mazie was proud to be wearing her new dress and equally proud to be in the presence of her Australian gentlemen Walter. Walter, ever the Giggle-mug, habitually wore a smile.

They decided to walk along the beach on their way back to the villa. Shortly, near the beach, they came upon a small native house with several horses. Walter greeted an elderly man and young boy grooming the horses. "Good day to ya."

In return, they happily offered, "Bonjour Monsieur and Mademoiselle."

Walter asked, "Would it be possible to borrow ya horses for a few hours to ride along the beach? For a fee of course…"

The older man looked at the young man for a translation. The young boy spoke to the man in French. Words spoke back and forth between the two. The young boy smiled and nodded. "Oui Monsieur, my grandfather said you may rent the horses for five and a half Franks."

Walter nodded his agreement to their terms.

"What is your name, young man?

"Oui Monsieur, my name is Timéo." He offered in broken English. Timéo continued, "I will put saddles on horses."

Mazie spoke up. "Garcon Timéo, I do not need a saddle. Just a bridle."

Timéo gave her a questionable gaze, then smiled. "Oui Mademoiselle."

Joyfully Timéo got the horse ready and then handed Mazie and Walter the readied horse's reins.

Walter exchanged money, adjusted his horse's cinch, latigo, and stirrups, and promptly boosted himself into the saddle.

Then swiftly and naturally—gracefully Mazie swung herself up onto the horse's bare back.

Timéo had never seen a man, yet a woman swing onto a horse's back with such ease and grace. Timéo, laughed and smiled at Mazie.

Walter smiled with pride at his stunning riding partner. "You ready?"

Mazie smiled and nodded. "Oui"

As they rode off together, Timéo ran after them, laughing and waving goodbye.

"Goodbye Timéo." Mazie returned.

They rode together slowly along the shore until they were out of sight of Timéo and the old man, then they quickened their pace to a full run, advancing into the shallow water of the ocean. Both riders soulfully burst into hysterical laughter as their horses splashed wildly through the ocean waves. Playfully, they scampered through water becoming soaking—wet.

Breathlessly, they stopped near a half-buried log on the shoreline. Laughing together, they dismounted, and tethered their steeds to the log. Water was filled with enjoyment and said, "This is so fun." Then added laughing, "This is a stack of cupcakes."

Mazie was still laughing, "Funny man, yes this is so much fun."

Walter embraced her and gave her a kiss.

"Mazie, I know ya have never been in the ocean before. What do ya think of her?"

Mazie smiled, "Mmm, this is wonderful" She took her wet finger and tasted the water. "It's so salty!" Bravely, she walked deeper into the water, until she was at waist level." Twirling around, with her hands skimming the water.

Walter sat in shallow water, watching her every move and enjoying the moment of this majestic site before him. "God, if you made any woman better than her, you must have kept her for yourself."

Mazie was awe-struck by the power of each wave that pulsated with authority from the sea. Each surging wave invigorated her. She stayed in the water enjoying its wonder, then returned to sit next to Walter and placed a sweet kiss on his forehead.

"My funny man, will you teach me how to swim someday?"

"I would love to."

They stayed and played in the water for a short while, then got back on their horses. They rode side by side along through the shallow edge of the shore. Their clothing was dripping wet when they returned the horses to Timéo.

"Ta, thank ya Timéo for letting us use ya horses." Walter said.

Timéo was enjoying these foreigners. "Oui, Monsieur. It was my pleasure." Politely and shyly, he asked. "Where are you from?"

Walter and Mazie handed him their horse's reins. Walter claimed, well I am from Australia, and this amazing Mademoiselle is from the United States of America." Continuing to add to the bravo, "In fact, she is a great American Indian from the high mountains of New Mexico. That's why she can ride so amazing."

"Woah!" Timéo was in awe. "So nice to have met you, Mademoiselle. Do you know Buffalo Bill Cody and Chief Sitting Bull?" Nodding his head continuously.

Mazie smiled and thought to herself how wonderful and pure was this boy who didn't host any prejudice.

Walter and Mazie walked quietly along the shoreline back to their villa.

Upon returning from the beach, Mazie decided she'd take a shower. She left the bathroom room door open. Walter lay naked on the bed watching her in a daze. Mazie adjusted the water to her needs, then playfully let the towel fall from her body.

Walter's cock swizzled with excitement at the beautiful image she left in his mind as she stepped behind the shower curtain. She began humming.

The thought of her wet naked body lingered in his mind, which intrigued him.

Mazie playfully stuck her wet upper body out from behind the curtain, in a way that would provoke the most charitable of saints. Her hair was wet and slicked back, the water glistening off her breasts, her nipples perky and inviting.

"Hey, Funny Man! I could use some help here." She threw a wet washcloth at Walter. Her slender forefinger beckoned him to come join her. "Come here." She said making it sound like an order.

Walter waltzed into the bathroom. His muscular frame towered to her side. Intrigued by her invitation, his cock surged to arousal. He stepped into the shower with her. "Yes, Ma'am what can I do for ya?"

Mazie pressed her wet naked body up against him and gave him a sweet longing kiss, her tongue teasing his senses.

"Well, my Funny Man, the first thing you can do is stop calling me ma'am."

"I call you that because you are a lady, and it's out of the respect you deserve."

Thinking to herself, I don't think I've ever been considered a lady. But I'll take that compliment. Kissing him again teasing him. "My Funny Man, surely you can come up with a loving nickname for the occasion? Hmmm?"

'Hmm, how about A-Mazie, because you are so amazing?"

She laughed.

Walter stood under the shower with his powerful frame clinging to hers, the water spraying over their embrace. He found her perplexing and tantalizing.

She kissed him slow and sweetly at first then with zeal and passion, as her tongue flickered in his month.

Walter groaned his approval, "Mmm, Mazie, ya are such a beautiful woman." Joking, "Ya, make this Aussie lightheaded because all my blood is flowing to my donger."

Mazie responded with her eyes flashing—teasing. "Well, at least you didn't call me ma'am this time." She softly sucked the water from his chest, gently nibbling on his nipples. Then giggling.

Walter playfully responded. "Dear one, are you teasing me?" He could feel the silhouette of her slender feminine outline. His hand traveled up and down her back with his hands resting on her soft ass.

Giggling, she began humming. Looking up to his face she then laughed at his amused expression.

Walter's eyes followed her, watching her, studying her body for a moment, how her wet-silky black hair flowed down her back. He observed her smile and then realized that he was smiling too. Their kiss started slow and tender, then turned into that of ravishment. Then he began nibbling onto her ears, neck, and shoulders. He turned her away from him and sucked the water from her back. Trailing his tongue down to the small of her back, nipping and sucking the water from her silky skin. Never could he imagine skin tasting so sweet.

Mazie made an inward hiss from the pleasure she

received. She backed her body up to his cock, pressing her buttocks on him, teasing him to the petals of her womanly wildflower, inviting him to enter her. Walter gently entered from behind her, slowly burying his length inside the cave of her womanhood.

Mazie gasped from his fill within her. "Oh My… Funny Man… Damn, this is good." She bucked back at him, swallowing him deep within her.

He could feel the water caressing them as he drove in and out. He placed one hand on her hip to guide his thrust. His other hand explored her breasts, playing with her sweet flesh and tweaking her nipples. Soon, the slow mastering thrust turned to ravishment. They humped hard and fast, the sexual energy building to a peek. She threw herself back to greet him with each plunge. He felt capable of going on forever, filling her with his strength. Onward, their momentum joined together with a wild, enigmatic rhythm. Until their erotic appetite was teamed up and totally satisfied.

He gently turned her toward him and embraced her. Upon his breast, she buried her face and clung to him. He felt the softness of her, and the warmth and quick heave of her breasts. Her heart echoed his. He whispered to her. "Mazie…" Unable to finish his words, he kissed her tenderly.

After their shower, Mazie and Walter wrapped themselves in a blanket again and went out to sit on the porch. Her bedraggled state gave her an earthly quality that Walter found incredibly sexy and her lush—raw beauty was becoming more and more difficult to ignore. Walter grabbed the champagne from their basket and brought it along with two glasses to the porch. Their hearts were filled with smiles as they clinked their glasses together in a silent toast.

They didn't know just how special this bottle of Champagne was that Adeline had given to them. Lanson—Champagne was a very old and cherished maker of Champagne in the Champagne region of Rheims near where they were based. Lanson had given many very expensive bottles to some military personnel fighting for France in order to make space in the cellars to shelter and protect their local towns' people.

Watching the ocean waves, all of a sudden, Mazie bursts into laughter.

Walter questioned, "What is so amusing my amazing—Amazie?

"No, no, I just realized my ex-husband, Junior, didn't have a clue when it came to pleasing a woman."

"Well, it's a well-known fact that most Yankee blokes like Junior, don't have the proper blood flow necessary to please Shelia's the way they should be pleased."

Mazie continued to giggle.

* * *

It was slowly turning to dusk as they sat silently watching the ocean. She could smell him, clean, soaped, and warm, his hair, shiny from its recent wash. She felt a sense of peace wash over her as he smiled. She gave him a light kiss, then wrapped herself within his powerful frame. He felt the softness of her, and her warmth, and the quick heave of her soft, bare breast. A lifetime of feeling and searching and reflecting came together for them at that moment. And Walter knew it was pure love that he had found with Mazie. And in the catch of the same moment, she fell in love with him, with the spell from that love never to be broken between them. Could anything interfere? For there was a stronger power from the divine working here.

Suddenly, their joy melted as they watched two large waves of thirty or more British and US Dehavilland Bombers warplanes fly over them, undoubtedly heading to the front.

Walter shook his head in disgust, "Holy shit would you look at that." Laughing, "That my dear, translates to the English word of "KA-BOOM" behind German lines."

# Chapter 26

As the saying goes, "All quiet on the Western Front, with an armistice in order, there was much peace at Fort Champagne. After discovering that Remy was no longer at Saint Mary's, Mazie and Walter took the opportunity to write letters and visit several orphanages in hopes of locating Remy. They even asked for help from their adversary Fort Champagnes, British Commander, Lieutenant Colonel Jernigan's support, to see if he could get the nuns at Saint Mary's to tell him where they had sent Remy. Lieutenant Colonel Jernigan felt guilty, having caused the boy's removal from the Fort, and he agreed to help. Weeks of searching, inquiries, and letters sent were all to no avail. No one could find Fort Champagne's Boy Remy.

The mail truck had just arrived, and both Watler and Mazie received letters, so they ran to their secret wine cellar to read their letters together.

"I got a letter from my brother Emiliano!" Mazie was so grateful to hear from him.

"Go ahead, you read your first," Walter said.

"Damn! It was taken four months for this letter to get to me." The letter reported that Emiliano had received a commission from William Frisch, a wealthy businessman from Boston. Mr. Frisch loved the trill and mysteries of archaeology, and he was going to donate his findings to New Mexico State University. Emiliano believed strongly that all of the artifacts found in New Mexico should stay in New Mexico. Emiliano fought against removing of New Mexico's artifacts, which were shipped away to Harvard, Yale, or the Smithsonian, then stored or displayed in their own museums. Emiliano respected and trusted William Frisch and enjoyed working for him. They had recently discovered, unearthed, and recorded the findings of a small Mimbres village near La Palomas, New Mexico. Emiliano was equally excited that he would earn enough money to enroll in college at the New Mexico State Archaeology Department in the upcoming Fall.

As she read the letter out loud to Water, she beamed with happiness and love.

"Walter, please read your letter."

"Ta! I bloody will, but I am not sure whose return address this is or who it is from." He held it up to the light hoping for some magical hint to its contents. "It is postmarked 3rd Street in Wagga-Wagga, Straya." Furphy, who could it be from?" Walter opened the letter and started to read it out loud.

"*Dear Maj. Walter Andrew Thompson,*

*It is with respect and deepest sympathy that I inform you your parents Ian and Agnes Thompson, have died in an automobile accident.*"

*His face went pale. Horrified, he stopped reading it out loud. His hands were shaking as he continued reading his letter to himself.*

*They were returning from Wagga-Wagga at night on Motorway A20 when they hit a Kangaroo. The impact forced your parent's vehicle off the road, and their vehicle overturned, resulting in their death. Your neighbor Beatrice Hutchins has taken it upon herself to execute a bond-in-trust naming you an owner at a local parish bank to oversee any legal and financial matters until the time of your return.*

*Beatrice Hutchins has also placed her most trusted Aborigine help, Henry and Matilda, who expressed a deep fondness and respect for you, to work diligently to maintain things as they should at your family station until your return. Formal memorial services will take place upon your return home under your guidance and wishes.*

*Respectfully,*

*Magistrate Michael Sullivan*

*Wagga Wagga Parish, New South Wales*

Mazi gasped when she heard the first part of the letter and waited patiently for Walter to stop reading.

Walter put down the letter and embraced Mazie. Mazie sat with Walter to comfort him as he wept.

Later after calming their spirits, they went to the dining hall, when a British Courier tacked down Walter with another Letter. Walter and Mazie opened the letter and read it out loud together.

*To honor exemplary leadership,*

*To the lead Commander of Australian Light Horse Cavalry and Base commander of outpost Fort Champagne, region of Champagne, France, I King George V, House of Windsor, request the immediate yet temporary assignment of Maj. Walter Thompson, Doctor of Veterinarian Medicine to the Buckingham Royal Stables.*

*Major Thompson's exemplary academic achievements while attending Sydney University School of Veterinarian Medicine, battlefield heroics, and a glowing reference by the distinguished American war hero Colonel George Patton have placed Maj Thompson at the top of my list to oversee the care of the Royal Stables in preparation of the King's Parade to be held April 11, 1919.*

*While in the service of the Royal Stables, Maj Thompson will be under orders to communicate his duties to the Commander of the Australian Light Horse Cavalry. While here his rank and experience will be recognized, and he will not be requested to perform any duty outside of those by his current Commander.*

*George R.I*

"Crikey! Well, my amazing Mazie girl, it looks like I am heading to England tomorrow."

Walter was excited…

Mazie was apprehensive…

* * *

Walter traveled to the British Command Port Authority at Calais, presented his letter from the King, and was immediately ushered onto the overcrowded Queens Ship Tilda. It felt good for Walter to be at sea. Even though it was a brisk day, he stayed out on the VIP deck. When he went to sit in a deck chair. Walter approached a small, sinewy-looking Native

American man in US Army uniform, sitting in a deck chair. Walter asked him, "Mind if I join you, Mate?"

"Happy to have company. Have a seat."

The two men shook hands and exchanged names.

"Major Thompson of the Austrian Light Horse Regiment, but please don't worry about those fancy titles. Just call me Walter."

"Hunter Yazzie, United States Army."

"Good on ya. Where are ya from, Mate?

"I am from Ni'iijíhí, New Mexico, of the United States of America." Smiling, he added, white men call it Navajo, New Mexico.

"Ace! How about that! My girlfriend is from Mimbres, New Mexico."

"Ah, we are on opposite ends of the state. Mimbres is about 300 miles south of Ni'iijíhí."

"My girl, Mazie, is in the US Cavalry." Walter beamed proudly.

"The Mimbres are a proud people." He added, "I know of your woman. We met a few months ago in Fort Champagne. She is called Horse Girl."

"That's right! I was there the day when your Brigade came through the fort."

The two men talked the entire four-hour voyage across the English Channel. Walter learned that Hunter was on his way to England to be honored and to ride in the King's parade. He was representing the United States Indian Nations Code Talkers.

The United States Indian Nations "Code Talkers" were used to transmit encrypted messages during The Great War. In 1917, Commander Daniel Lecoq of the 142nd Infantry Regiment, 36th Division, assembled Native Americans to communicate in their indigenous languages to keep Allied plans secret. The Germans had already deciphered every previous American code but never could break the American Indian soldiers' "code." Native American languages lacked equivalent words for specific military terms like "machine gun" and "grenade," allowing the Code Talkers to improvise with their existing words and phrases to send coded messages. The valuable service of the Code Talkers saved countless American and Allied lives at a time when the American government discouraged and punished Native Americans for speaking their native language back in America.

The information Hunter shared with Walter fascinated Walter; he learned that the First Battalion was called one grain-corn. The Second Battalion was two-grain corn, and so on. The word for Company was bow; Machine Gun was little gun shoot fast; Artillery was big gun; Ammunition was arrows; Grenade-stone; Patrol-many scouts; gas-bad air; and Casualties were scalps.

* * *

Upon arriving at Dover, Walter reported to the Port of Entry Command Center. Walter told the official that he was traveling with a comrade and Hunter was to travel with him; they were then escorted in an Austin Officers Motorcar to Buckingham Palace, where he was presented to the Palace Liaison.

# Chapter 27

It was a sleepy, overcast day. A light snowfall was twirling and dancing to the ground without gaining much accumulation. Mazie found herself pining over Walter and wondering when he would return. With the war at armistice, would she be transferred to another location, or sent home? She worried and pondered if she would be ordered to report to another post and never see him again. And the vision of the nuns at Saint Mary's orphanage replayed repeatedly in her mind. She kept hearing the sister screaming, "You are an evil heathen and you will never see Master Remy again." Where had the nuns sent Remy too?" The questions of whether she would ever see Remy or Walter again haunted her. She found herself swimming in worries and was being trampled by a stampede of emotions.

She decided to take Hercules out for a ride to help calm her mind.

She left a note on her bed that she was going for a ride to the northwest woods near the Eu des Ermites.

Her ride through the woods reminded her of her many horseback adventures she had taken back home in Mimbres.

The Great War was under a peace agreement for the moment, and it was presumed that it would be over for good. Mazie pondered over the top Commanders of this Great War who were high on war, whether or not they would be able to obtain peace. She stopped to say a prayer, "Dear God, I pray for peace to end this war." Gosh! She thought about how many hundreds of thousands of prayers and cries God had heard during this war. There had been prayers from the French and her allies… And for every prayer, there had to have been a counter-prayer from the German soldiers. It would have been impossible for God to know who to help. Mazie let out a cleansing sigh! "Right now, Dear God, I only prayed for peace.

The beauty and splendor of riding amongst the mesmerizing light swirling snowflakes was calming her mind. She lost track of time and how far out she had traveled and suddenly realized she had ridden well beyond the wooded area where she usually rode.

* * *

Weeks earlier, there had been a horrid battle along the Ru de Bastourne River. It had been a harsh, dark, deadly storm going through the farmland and vineyards for days. What was left of the once pristine, countryside, was now an eerie disfiguration of mud beds from bomb-shelled graters, slit trenches and blisters, and remaining puddles of blood from the slaughter. The aftermath was filthy and spooky beyond belief.

As Mazie overlooked the area, she got chills. She quickly turned Hercules around and started to ride back into the woods when she heard a succession of gunfire from out of the woods. Her body convulsed into a second-by-second choreography as Hercules reared up at the sudden noise and was hit in the temple by gunfire. He instantly fell dead to the ground, trapping her left leg and hip underneath his mammoth body.

Her shocked nervous system sent a bolt of alarm to her mind when she realized that she could not get out from under Hercules, instinctively, Mazie reached for her pistol as she saw a German Gefreiter coming toward her. She lay still, waiting for the soldier to come closer, hoping he would think she was hit by his gunfire.

He was whistling an eerie tune as he approached her. He must have been confident with his kill because he had slung his German rifle over his shoulder. She could see he was having to strain his eyes, as his eyes seemed glazed-over and blank with extreme fatigue and madness from the war. It was impossible to tell the German soldier's age since the pureness of youth never lasted in their faces for very long from their reminiscences of war, but she could see he was very young.

He stopped his whistling and was smiling. It was a strange, ironic death-enthralled smile. It was the kind of smile that verged on the uncontrollable giggles of the insane. It was common for Gefreiters to come pillage and take the personal effects and weapons of their dead enemies as souvenirs or to sell.

Mazie's senses were working like strobes as the German soldier leaned toward her, getting ready to scavenge her personal effects. With a quick jolt of adrenaline, she aimed her pistol and shot the young soldier in his torso three times. He struggled to stay on his feet and staggered five yards away; he jerked and twitched, and then he fell lifeless to the ground. Mazie let out a war cry and then screamed. "The fucking war is over you asshole, we are under Armistice." She began sobbing, "You killed my Hercules." She then added in a mere whisper. "And I just killed a young man who should have had years yet to his life."

Fear bombarded her as the blood ran out of Hercules. Again, she tried to get out from under Hercules, but with the adrenaline now worn off, a sharp pain shot through her body and she passed out.

* * *

When Mazie came to, it was dawn, and with it, the realization of her situation. She had no water, and more importantly, no way of getting out from under Hercules. As she scouted her surroundings, she had a disturbing, grotesque kind of delirium looking at the river, forest, countryside, and hills, and she started thinking about the death and mythos that would be held there for years to come. The Fall leaves scattered the muddy, blood-soaked ground. In the middle of the field there was a mound of ash from where they burned the dead. She saw some of the ash blow and entwined with the brilliance of whimsical virgin snowflakes. It was beauty swirling and dancing with abhorrent death.

She tried praying and chanting with the hopes and belief that someone would find her. Surely someone from Fort Champagne would be looking for her. "Maybe my Walter will find me?"

She was cold... So cold... She was thirsty, her mouth was dry, and she kept working her lips futilely to ease the dryness.

Mazie remembered sitting at the kitchen table with Emiliano as her father read a verse of Psalm from the Bible. She said the Psalm passage out loud. "The Lord is my light and my salvation, whom shall, I fear? The Lord is the stronghold of my life, of whom shall I be afraid? When the wicked advance against me to devour me, it is my enemies and my foes who will stumble and fall?"

A bolt of pain raged through her leg, and she called out to the heavens. "Dear God, be with me now. I need you now." And she struggled to complete the bible passage. "One thing I ask from the Lord, this only do I seek, that I may dwell in the house of the Lord all the days of my life."

Suddenly, she wished she had learned more of that passage. She noticed a hawk flying over her, and knew it was a sign from the Spirit world. She called out, "Hawk, please go bring me help." She watched with a glimmer of hope as it glided out of site toward fort Champagne. Whispering she plead, "Please... Go bring me help... Please.

* * *

Hours later, as dusk ebbed into the night, her despair set in, and she sobbed as optimism no longer sprang from her. She cried until she no longer had a voice and fainted into a deep somatic sleep.

"Tedda Aruka, my Granddaughter, you have entered the Spirt World."

Mazie didn't question who she was with. Even though she had never met him, she knew he was her mother's father; she knew he was her grandfather. He was speaking in their native tongue, and she clearly understood everything he was telling her.

Her Grandfather went on, "Our creator has given you many gifts in your lifetime. You are a Sage... You have a spiritual connection with horses. You are an enchanter of horses. Tedda Aruka, this is why you are called Horse Girl. You must share that power."

Mazie marveled at her radiant vision; her grandfather was majestic, joyous, and stunning.

He humbly added, "You are a decedent of the bravest people below the spirit world. You must feed your spiritual hunger and learn."

In a flash, Mazie's heightened senses were suddenly looking down on sacred Mother-Earth, where she could see herself lying lifeless and trapped beneath her beloved Hercules.

She was not alarmed by the vision... She was calm...

With undeniable trust, she asked, "Grandfather, is it my time to join my ancestors and return to the Spirit World?"

"No Tedda Aruka, it is not your time. You will not follow in my footsteps to the Spirit World." He shook his head no.

Continuing, he added, "The land is ripe with the stories of our people. If you listen on a still night, you can hear their voices, their chants, and their cries."

Mazie queried, "When I was a child, my mother told me how you died in a great battle against the people of the Mescalero."

Grandfather lowered his head in remorse. "It is shameful that I did not honor all life. I had an ego filled with a thirst for power, and I was too eager for battle. I was stuck by my enemies' arrows. And I too, was trapped under my horse, dwindled and left my earthly existence."

Mazzie suddenly had a vision of her grandfather dead and lying beneath his horse.

Grandfather added, "There are many who do not regard living people and animals as sacred entities. You must help to change this. You have much work to do. And, you must stay to love and heal Mother Earth's creatures and teach mankind to honor and respect them.

"Mother Earth is ripe with the stories and lessons of all people. If you listen on a still night, you can hear their voices, their chants, their cries, and their stories. You must learn from these stories."

"You must go back now. You must heal yourself with the light of the sun and the rays of the moon. Listen closely to the sounds of the rain, the sounds of the waterfall, and the swaying of the trees. Watch and listen, and let calmness claim you, and you will heal."

"May you walk in beauty, Tedda Aruka." He smiled, and his beautiful presence faded away.

# Chapter 28

Mazie was aroused by a loud noise. She woke up dizzy and with extreme vertigo. She could not ever recall feeling so drained… so weak. "Where am I?", she asked as she looked around. She first noticed her leg strung up in a strange apparatus. She was stiff and sore beyond belief, which forced her to move her head slowly as she looked around the room. Again, in a weak scratchy voice, she said, "Where am I?" Mazie felt like she had been sleeping for days, and her body ached and was woeful as she finally came to the realization that she was in a hospital. Weariness crept into her senses. With her voice straining and cracking, she called out as loud as she could, "Where am I?"

A nurse dressed in a bright white uniform heard her cry and came to her bedside. She spoke in French, and Mazie could not understand her. "Sorry, but, I do not speak French."

"Oh! Chéri, you are finally awake." She sweetly patted Mazie's head. "I will go get Docteur."

Mazie's fatigue grew as she waited, anticipating someone to return, for it seemed like hours before anyone came. After a lengthy time, the nurse who had been there earlier returned with a doctor. Looking over the top of his glasses, he took Mazie's hand and said with a strong French accent, "Lieutenant Atencio, I am glad you have finally come to."

Clearing his throat, he questioned her, "Do you remember that your horse had fallen on top of you, and you were trapped for two days?

Mazie skimmed through her memory, and her memory took shape. She started to cry for the loss of Hercules. Tearfully, she answered, "Yes, my horse Hercules was gunned down by a German soldier, and I could not get out from under him."

"Yes, after you were found missing at Fort Champagne, a patrol was assembled to find you. A Red-Skin…" Correcting his words he continued, "An American Indian soldier found you and took you to the nearby field hospital. When Fort Champagnes Commander discovered that you had suffered injuries, he immediately transferred you here at the Hôtel-Dieu Paris Hospital." Patting her shoulder, he added, "The words "lucky, to be alive, do not even apply." Shaking his head in disbelief, he said, "Lieutenant, it is a miracle that you are still alive."

The Doctor called out some orders in French to the attending nurse, and she quickly scurried away.

"Allow me to introduce myself; I am Docteur Dominique Jean Larrey. And it has been my privilege to working on the famous "Horse Girl"." Laughing, he added, "Your disappearance and injuries have made quite a stir in the equestrian community."

Mazie looked at her leg. She was still confused and asked, "What is this thing attached to my leg?"

"It is called a Thomas Splint. It is there to help stabilize your broken leg." Looking over her chart, he said. "I am glad you finally came to. You need a lot of rest now. I will have water and chicken broth brought to you. You arrived to us very dehydrated. I encourage you to eat and drink. I will give you more information when I return."

Mazie released a big sigh, and said with scratchy voice. "Thank You, Doctor."

Docteur Dominique Larrey was well aware of the medical research and science of the 20th century which had progressed from the gruesome medical practices since the beginning of the war. Whereas before, a battlefield leg injury such as Mazie's had a high likelihood of resulting in death. However, most injured combatants have now survived their injuries with modern advances in orthopedic surgery.

Most Doctors assigned to Battlefields used all the available medical chemical resources to prevent infection.

They had a number of alternative methods. It was a common practice to use antibacterial Resorscin and Camphor on and around the wound, along with the practice of 'debridement' – whereby the tissue around the wound was cut away and the wound sealed, it was a common way to prevent infection.

Later that evening, Docteur Dominique Larrey came back to check on Mazie. With a thick French accent, he explained to her, "Lieutenant Atenco, it was most fortunate that the Commander sent you here to us." He pulled up a chair next to her bed and continued. "It is your broken leg that will require extensive treatment. Broken legs often take several months to heal and will require hours of therapy, rest, and recuperation. I have just scheduled for you several regiments of treatment. Massage, physiotherapy, and electrical therapy are some treatments we will provide for you. The Hôtel-Dieu Paris Hospital is one of the best places in the world to convalesce from an injury."

It took all she had of her composer not to giggle at his funny French accent and how he pronounced some of his words. "Thank you, Doctor. I am grateful for your care and will do my best to recover quickly."

* * *

Docteur Dominique Larrey was thankful for the ongoing Armistice, inasmuch he had witnessed far too many life-ending injuries from the war and far too many grotesque injuries that required more surgery, months of physiotherapy, and often necessary amputations. Disgustingly, during wartime the main object of the treatment was to get the men back to the war front as quickly as possible. Or to ensure that they were "invalided" out' as fit as possible. Which meant they were awarded a minor pension so that they did not cost their country a lot of money. As a reward for their service, artificial limbs were provided to war veterans for free. However, one British report suggested that men were unwilling to use the cumbersome artificial limbs that were provided by the state, preferring to use crutches and a much lighter peg leg instead. Many men left the war with permanent disabilities and wounds that made them unable to return to their pre-war employment.

In the battle field, wounds to the extremities were often so severe that many thousands of soldiers had to immediately have their limbs amputated. In France, they used the same vintage guillotine to amputate limbs that had been used to cut off heads during the French Revolution. As traumatic as it was, amputation saved the lives of many men as it often prevented infection.

* * *

A week went by and Mazie got a surprise visit from Adeline. "Hi, Angel!" She said excitingly. She squeezed Mazie so hard Mazie wanted to yelp from the pain. "You sure gave us all quite the scare." Hugging her again, "Oh, it is oh-so-wonderful to see you."

Mazie sat up in bed as much as the splint would allow her to. "I have so many questions about how I got here to a hospital in Paris. Who found me? Have you heard from Walter?"

Adeline giggled, "Hold your ponies' girl! You remember the Native American battalion that came through Fort Champagne last fall?"

"Yes, of course."

"Well, they came back though the day you went missing. And one of those redskins tracked you down." She shook her head. "God only knows how they can do that…"

"And?" Mazie was getting impatient for the answer about Walter.

"Anyways… He found you just in the nick of time. When he brought you back to the Fort Lieutenant Colonel Jernigan and I personally rushed you here to the hospital." Whining she continued. "I was so worried about you. I stayed here with you for a couple of days, waiting for you to recover from unconsciousness. But before that happened, I was sent back to the Fort." Again, she hugged Mazie.

"And Walter? Have you heard from Walter? Does he know I am here?"

Adeline started to whine again, "No… I sent him several letters, and Lieutenant Colonel Jernigan even sent him a telegram."

Mazie's heart sank.

"What about Remy? Has anyone found which orphanage he was transferred too? Tearing up Mazie flashed back to the memory of the way Remy mispronounced orphanage.

Adeline shook her head no. "No, no word as to where those beastly nuns sent Remy to." Now she too was crying. "But we are not giving up. We are all trying to locate him."

* * *

Mazie spent many afternoons with Docteur Dominique Larrey, and he insisted that she call him Dominique. It turned out that he had studied at Harvard Medical School in Massachusetts. And Dominique and the Prime Minister of France George Clemenceau, were friends. It had been the Prime Minister who arranged for Mazie's continual care at Hôtel-Dieu Paris. Mazie had become quite the celebrity in the equestrian world, and many were concerned for her wellbeing. Dominique also had a love of horses and continually asked Mazie questions and advice about his own horses.

* * *

Mazie spent many days resting outside in her wheelchair when the weather was acceptable. Even though it was winter, Mazie enjoyed sitting outside bundled up in blankets. She found peace in the light snow and the birds fluttering about. One afternoon, she had another visit from Adeline. She enjoyed spending time with her and catching up with the news and happenings back at Fort Champagne. She continually found herself smiling and laughing with Adeline. She thought some people just make you feel better when you are around them. Walter quickly came to mind. Yes, he made her feel happy. He was the sunshine to her soul and medicine for her mind. She was becoming increasingly troubled. Walter, where are you?

* * *

Mazie worked arduously toward her recovery. She worked diligently through her physical therapy sessions and listened to any and all advice on how to heal quickly. She continually told herself that every step was an opportunity for another miracle and every day was a gift from God. Every breath was a privilege denied by many in this war.

* * *

After two months of treatment and hours of physical therapy, it wasn't before long before Mazie was able to walk with crutches, then eventually a cane. Her body was healing and getting stronger, yet her mind was becoming clouded from continual worry. There still had not been any word from Walter.

While Mazie was sitting in the hospital garden, a young lad was nearby riding by on a petite, spirited horse. Mazie could see he was having trouble controlling the steed. With the aid of her cane, she hobbled over to him. "Young man, may I see your horse?"

"Oui!" He rode his horse over to Mazie, while the horse skittishly jumped and jerked about.

Mazie gleamed with love for the animal. She rubbed his face, then slowly moved around the horse, limping her every step, suddenly unaware of her injuries. Speaking in her native tongue, she spoke with a soothing, cooing tone.

Mazie continued for several minutes to move her hand over the horse's back and legs It was pure loving reiki to the horse. The horse's response to her was astonishing, he instantly became pacified and subdued. It was as if the horse and Mazie were in an ethereal trance.

Dominique was walking nearby and stopped to watch Mazie's bewitching interaction with the horse. He watched in awe and inspiration. Vexed, he slowly walked up to Mazie and the horse. "Mazie, your interaction with this horse is supernatural." Shaking his head in disbelief, he then said in French. "Simplement magnifique!"

The lad who owned the horse stood with his mouth open and repeated in a daze. "Oui! Simplement magnifique!"

* * *

By the third week of March, Mazie could walk with only the aid of a cane and was waiting for her hospital discharge papers from the US Cavalry. She could tell that Dominique was sweet on her, and she was flattered. However, her heart was heavy from missing Walter and wondering and continual worry as to why she had not heard from him.

Dominique received a letter from one of his old college friends in London, England and had been personally invited him to the upcoming King's Parade to honor those who fought and died in the Great War. He showed Mazie the invitation. "Mazie, will you come with me to the King's Parade? It promises to be a surprenant événement. And I am sure you would enjoy watching all the Kings grand horses in the Parade."

Mazie pondered over his invitation. She wasn't really interested in seeing the King's parade. Yet, she did want to see the horses. And she was certainly ready to get out of this hospital. Oh my God, she thought, London is the last place she knew of Walters whereabouts.

# Chapter 29

When Walter first arrived, he was excited to work with the King's horse. He was first sent to Sandringham, where the majority of King George's personal horses were kept. He stayed busy for months tending to the horses, training the staff, and consulting with the King's veterinarian. Repeatedly, Walter went back and forth to work with the Royal Mews at Buckingham Palace, Rotten Row, Hyde Park, and again back to the country estates at Sandringham. Routinely, Walter sent letters to Mazie. He missed her, and his heart ached for her. As the weeks went by, he missed her more and more, and in each letter, he wrote to her, he increasingly professed his love. He worried and thought it queer that he had not heard back from Maize. He spent many an hour keeping himself busy to muffle his worries.

Opposite the Buckingham Palace Gardens in Central London were the Royal Mews of Buckingham Palace. They were directly responsible for the road travel arrangements for the King and members of the Royal Family. The Royal Mews tended to everything from horses to carriages. Walter enjoyed working with the Royal Mews, they were extremely modern and had the most advanced equipment, their progressive veterinarian sciences and procedures were highly respected throughout the equestrian world.

* * *

By the month of April, Walter still had not heard from Mazie and was anxious to have the King's Parade over so he could return to Fort Champagne to see her.

Countless hours were spent with hundreds of people to organize the King's Parade; it was sure to be a grand event. Walter's driver was taking him from Sandringham back to Buckingham Palace. As Walter was daydreaming about Mazie, they passed a motorcar pulling into the driveway. Shaking his head, "Furphy," He said to himself, "that woman in that car looked like Mazie. Oh, Crikey! I am missing her so much that I am going mad."

Dominique had sweet-talked Mazie into traveling to England. Trying to allure Mazie, he had arranged for the finest of accommodations the entire trip. She was grateful for the opportunity to see England and was looked forward to seeing the King's horses in the parade. However, she really wasn't comfortable with all the opulence that surrounded her.

Dominique had prearranged for Mazie to tour the Sandringham's stables. When they entered the arena, they were met by the Stable Master Reginald Abingdon and three of the Stable Yeomen dressed in the Royal Stable's impeccable work uniforms. Mazie hadn't seen such shiny black boots on men since she was back in Fort Sam Houston at dinner with Colonel Patton, who at that time was a Captain. The arrogance that they greeted her with made her feel small. As Dominique introduced Mazie to the men, they looked down at the end of their noses at her and responded with a weak handshake.

One of the Stable-equerry was exercising one of their many well-bred horses in the arena. Her curiosity and the need to be away from the snobby men, she inquired, "May I see the horse that gentleman is riding." As the horse drew near, she noticed that the horse was slightly out of step.

"Yes, of course." Hesitantly he said. The Stable Master summoned the horse and rider over to them, and the rider was excused. Mazie handed her cane to Dominique and ran her hands over the magnificent steed. As she spoke her native language to the horse, she noticed the Stable Master had rolled his eyes. Undisturbed, she sweetly talked to the horse, then asked, "May I ride him?"

'Ah… Young lady, this is a valuable and highly spirited steed and requires great skill."

Dominique interrupted him and said with confidence. "Trust me Monsieur Reginald Abingdon. She knows how to ride this horse."

Doubtful he agreed, "Very well, Doctor Larrey."

As customary, one of the stable men helped Mazie onto the well-polished English saddle. He adjusted the stirrups for her and handed her the reins.

Mazie started out slow and then quickly had the steed move into a graceful trot. On command, she was able to stop him instantly, then back up. She even had him spin in circles. Simultaneously, Mazie rode gracefully and well-poised. She was a true vision of equestrian perfection. And she was loving every minute of her exposition.

The Stable-Master and his men watched in awe. And Dominque gleamed with pride.

After several minutes, Mazie returned to the men; slowly and carefully she dismounted the horse so that she would not hurt her leg. She limped over to Dominique and retrieved her cane. Proudly, she said, "Thank you for allowing me to ride your magnificent horse. It was most enjoyable." Stopping, she then added. "Oh, by the way… You need to have your Farrier check his front right hoof." One of the Stable-Yeomen immediately went to the steed, lifted his hoof, and noticed a loose nail in the steed's shoe. He smiled and nodded at Mazie.

* * *

That Afternoon, Dominique and Mazie returned to Buckingham Palace to tour the Royal Stable of the Royal Mew. Dominique was busy conversing with the Duke of Windsor, so Mazie wandered off into the arena where they were getting ready for a meeting concerning the planning of the upcoming King's parade. Fifty or sixty men were standing around listening to the Parades Choreographers' instructions.

Walter was there listening intently, and his eyes roomed out over the crowd when he spotted a woman who looked like Mazie on the far side of the arena. He wasn't sure if he had really seen her. When she moved to the front of a group of Royal Mews, his heart sang and confirmed it was truly her.

Walter wanted to rush over to her, however, he couldn't break protocol. He felt like an anxious horse waiting at the gate of a horse race. He was not able to tune into and hear a word that was being said.

Walter anxiously watched Mazie from across the arena. Mazie finally took notice of Walter, and she beamed with joy. Walter gave her a slight wave and a huge smile. Both Walter and Mazie waited impatiently as they were trapped by the continual jabber of the choreographer and waited restlessly for the damn meeting to be over.

Seconds after the meeting was concluded Mazie and Walter ran to meet each other in the area. They embraced and fell into a loving kiss. It was a kiss that held more love than most people had ever experienced in their lifetime. The people around them were in awe over the whimsical sight of the two lovers and began clapping for them. Not wanting to let go they embraced each other for a long period of time. Their love ignited... Both had trouble talking and asking questions. In the heat of the moment, they only wanted to hold each other. God had truly answered each other's prayers.

* * *

Walter and Mazie spent the entire afternoon catching up with what had happened the last four months. Walter was saddened to hear of Mazie's horrific incident with Hercules being gunned down by the German soldier and the months of her recovery. Walter had been given a lead as to where Remy had been transferred. Walter received word that Remy might be at Saint Bernadettes Orphanage in Knockholt, located nearby southeast of London. Walter and Mazie planned to investigation the lead the following day after the parade.

* * *

Traditionally, every year in England, there would be the obligatory King's Parade in honor of the King's Birthday. However, this year, his Royal Highness King George the Fifth did not think it fair to celebrate his birthday with the usual pomp and circumstance. This celebration was to be a proper homecoming for the thousands of young soldiers who had returned from The Great War, and the many thousands of men who died. King George declared this year of 1919 would belong to England's military men, and their allies.

The day of the King's Parade was a stupendous event. Their hands embraced and intertwined lovingly together as Walter and Mazie stood with thousands of people there, watching the audacious cavalcade stream before them. Walter was happy and excited to see the parade, "Crikey! Mazie, I wish Remy was here to see this."

Mazie watched in disbelief as the fanfare passed by. She was overwhelmed by the ostentation of this pageantry, and the riches and gauche misuse of wealth. She thought, "I think their crowns have slipped over their eyes and have blinded them to see the needs of their people." She tried to understand and enjoy the beauty of the parade and not criticize. Mazie said a silent prayer. "Dear Lord, thank you for stopping the war. Thank you for finding my Walter. I am trying not to judge, but how can these people cherish a human king? You are the only King. The money spent here for this parade could be helping the needs of the families of the fallen and the broken. I do not understand this English tradition and love of their King. I pray that I will understand." Mazie was a true queen that knew she didn't need a golden gem inlaid crown, for her crown wasn't on her head but in her soul.

* * *

Leading the parade first came the dozens of active military men who had fought in the war, carrying the colors of their regiments, air squadrons, and naval fleets. Next was

The Royal Marching Band in full dress playing England's most patriotic anthems. Following, were fifteen Royal Cavalry Guards, with King George the Fifth on his personal steed dressed in his stunning opulent full-dress uniform. Close behind was the Queen in the gilded gold Royal Coach, followed was her protected four Commanders in Chiefs who represented the Navy, Army, Royal Air Force, and Marines. Flanked on either side of the regal Royal Coach were six valiant Mounted Royal Guards.

The parade started at Buckingham Palace then proceed up Grosvenor Place, and on to Hyde Park. At Hyde Park, waiting to fall into their assigned position in the parade would be the Duke of Windsor, The Duke of Gloucester, and The Duke of Kent. Each Duke was escorted by members of their royal family, Color Guards, and distinguished heroic Servicemen from the region that they resided over. Lastly was the Four Branches of The Service Representatives.

The parade then circled around through Trafalgar Square and Whitehall, where a memorial was under constructed to honor those who had given their lives in the tragic Great War. Flags flying at half-mast from America, Australia, New Zealand, India, Belgian, French, and the Flag from the United Kingdom. These flags did not move from the wind. These flags flew from the last breath of every soldier that collectively died defending their countries.

# Chapter 30

As their ship set out to sea, Walter and Mazie watched England's White Cliffs of Dover disappear in the distance. They were aboard the vessel Trans-Pacific RMS- Empress and headed out to Australia.

Water kissed Mazie, then said. "As soon as we get to Straya, I will buy you another Hercules."

Mazie laughed and repeated, "Straya!"

"Ace-Girl! You'll be talking Australian before ya know it."

Mazie's smile shined with gratitude, love, and joy.

Walter tightened his arms around Mazie and said, "There are over one billion people with smiles on this earth, and your smile is the only one that pours life into me."

"Mmm!" She smiled as her soul found comfort in his words and in his arms.

Just then, Remy came skipping up to them while he practiced saying Australia. "Australia… Australia… Australia…" Joining the hug, he put his small arms around Walter and Mazie.

Walter kissed the top of his head and questioned Remy, "Hey, little Mate! I've got a question for ya." How do dragons blow out candles?"

Remy shrugged his shoulders and laughed.

Happy tears filled their eyes. They laughed, and their souls merged together in their new life's journey…

* * *

The world breathed relief with the armistice concluding in peace. The Allied Armed Forces returned to their homes. Both Mazie and Walter had been discharged from their services. They found Remy at Saint Bernadette's Orphanage. Because of Walter's distinguished service and high rank, Walter secured legal custody and guardianship of Remy.

After arriving in Australia, Walter and Mazie had a sweet, modest wedding ceremony and were wed by the honorable and reverent Theadore Rador, on Bee-Bees ranch.

Walter and Mazie successfully completed Remy's adoption process, and merged into the loving Thompson family. A year later, Mazie gave birth to their daughter Anna, named after Mazie's mother. The Thompson family bought BeeBee's station and quickly became a legendary ranch known as the "Mimbres Station."

To this day, Remy Thompson is a celebrity amongst Australian horseman and is often described as the best horsemen in the history of the world. Remy Thompson had trained more horses and received tributes in more equestrian events than any horseman Australia has ever seen.

Four generations later, the Thompson family's "Mimbres Station" remains one of the great equine facilities in Australia. Great Nanna-Mazie's horsemanship techniques were recorded years ago, and are still used today. The Thompson family has trained more horses and received countless awards in all-around equestrian events. The Thompson family is respected in Australia and overseas as a Master Horseman for their achievements covering a wide variety of horsemanship disciplines including rodeo and campdrafting, and started training horses necessary for a station work.

The Thompson family's experience ranges from educating horse and riders for a wide client base, from starting colts, preparing sale horses, showing horses in halter, pleasure, trail, hunter, western riding, show hacks, stock horses, working cow horses, and reining and cutting.

Currently, Walter Thompson, known as Walt, who was named after his great-grandfather, has been inducted into the Australian Quarter Horse Association Hall of Fame. He is also a recipient of the National Cutting Horse Association Hall of Fame, and the Reining Australia Hall of Fame, he is a National Reining Horse Association Legend Rider, and he was recently inducted into the Furlong Stud Equine Hall of Fame in Toowoomba. In 2022 Walt received an Order of Australia Medal for his services to the equine industry.

The Thompson family now concentrate on Horse rescue and giving clinics in horsemanship for special needs children.

# History

We wrote this story for the forgotten faces of The Great War, which began on June 28th, 1914, and officially ended on the 11th hour of the 11th day of the 11th month of 1918, when finally, the incessant boom of artillery abruptly went silent along the Western Front in France. It was considered one of the deadliest global conflicts in history. WWI was fought between two coalitions, the Allied Forces who were primarily France, the United Kingdom, Russia, Italy, Japan and the United States, and the Central Powers who were led by Germany, Austria, Hungary, and the Turkish Ottoman Empire. Fighting occurred throughout Europe, the Middle East, Africa, the Pacific, and parts of Asia. An estimated 9 million soldiers were killed in combat, plus another 23 million wounded, while 5 million civilians died as a result of military action, hunger, and disease. Millions more died as a result of genocide, from the 1918 Spanish flu pandemic.

Eight million horses, donkeys and mules died in WWI, three-quarters of them died from the appalling conditions they worked in. After the war, most of the surplus horses were destroyed or sold to the French as work horses, or for meat.

The war ended with an armistice, an agreement in which both sides agree to stop fighting, rather than a surrender. For both sides, an armistice was the fastest way to end the war's misery and carnage.

By November 1918, both the Allies and Central Powers who'd been attacking each other for four years were pretty much out of strength both physically and mentally. German offensives that year had been defeated with heavy casualties, and in late summer and fall of 1918, the British, French and U.S. forces had pushed them steadily back. With the United States able to send more and more fresh troops into combat, the Germans were outmatched. Germany's allies crumbled around them as well, the war's outcome seemed clear. Four empires collapsed after WWI: Ottoman, Austro-Hungarian, German, and Russian.

U.S. troops fought their first battle of World War I on November 2, 1917, in the trenches at Barthelemont, France.

The greatest single loss of life in the history of the British army occurred during the Battle of Somme, when the British suffered 60,000 casualties in one day. More British men were killed in that one WWI battle than the U.S. lost from all of its armed forces and the National Guard combined.

WWI transformed the United Stated into the largest military power in the world. WWI brought a new era of warfare. The most significant development was air power, which brought civilians in the line of fire. By 1918, it was clear that the days of cavalry as a realistic fighting force were over with the introduction of poisonous gas. Tanks heralded a new era of offensive war. Finally, the Nazi blitzkrieg tactic of WWII grew out from the final Allied offensive of 1918 in which tanks, aircraft, artillery, and men were carefully coordinated.

The trench network of World War I stretched approximately 25,000 miles from the English Channel to Switzerland. The area was known as the Western Front. British poet Siegfried Sassoon wrote, "When all is done and said, the war was mainly a matter of holes and ditches."

January 1917 Germany -- under pressure from a British sea blockade – stepped up a campaign of attacking British merchant vessels with U-boat submarines, aiming to throttle the island. This pushed the United States to enter the conflict, angered by the torpedoing of neutral ships in the Atlantic and vessels carrying US citizens.

Washington declares war on Germany on April 6$^{th}$ 1917, and on 26$^{th}$ the June the first US deployment arrived at the French port of Saint-Nazaire.

The US involvement began in 1917. In May of 1917, the US Congress passed the conscription or draft meant to increase the size of the US Army. By the end of the war, 2.7 million men had been drafted. Another 1.3 million volunteered. Beyond price, the precious lives lost in WWI for the U.S. was 116,516. And the financial cost was more than $30 billion equal to $650 billion in the time of this writing.

**"Throughout the many ever-changing eras of history, men have learned how to win wars... Isn't it time men learn how to win peace."**

**-Amaia Joy**

# Bibliography

Gawani, Pony Boy. Horse Follow Closely: Native American Horsemanship. 1998, Bowtie Press

Herr, Michael, Dispatches, 1978, NY New York, Avon Books.

https://www.britannica.com/topic/Mimbres

https://www.fs.usda.gov/detail/gila/about-forest/?cid=stelprdb5037337

https://www.archaeology.org/issues/89-1305/features/738-mimbres-bowls-southwest-collapse-reorganization

https://www.archives.gov/publications/prologue/2016/winter/zimmermann-telegram

https://www.archives.gov/publications/prologue/2017/fall/tonys-lab

http://warfarehistorynetwork.com/

https://en.wikipedia.org/wiki/Hoboken,_New_Jersey

https://hudsonreporter.com/2017/04/30/hoboken-had-historic-role-in-the-war/

https://www.history.org.uk/student/resource/4512/american-dime-novels-1860-1915

https://www.alabama-coushatta.com/about-us/our-history/

https://en.wikipedia.org/wiki/Alabama%E2%80%93Coushatta_Tribe_of_Texas#Termination_efforts

https://en.wikipedia.org/wiki/File:Light_horse_walers.jpg

https://en.wikipedia.org/wiki/Horses_in_World_War_I

https://www.google.com/search?q=opi+commercial+with+horse&ie=UTF-8&oe=UTF-8&hl=en-us&client=safari

https://www.archives.gov/publications/prologue/2016/winter/zimmermann-telegram

*National Archives, Records of the American Expeditionary Forces (World War I)*

https://www.awmlondon.gov.au/australians-in-wwi

https://www.co.ozaukee.wi.us/789/Lighthouse

World War I – Wikipedia Web


https://cdnsm5s13.sharpschool.com/UserFiles/Servers/Server_251181/File/Durand%20History/19th%20Century/Mary%20Clemenceau%20Marries%20French%20Premier.pdf

https://en.wikipedia.org/wiki/Arabian_horse

https://www.thedonkeysanctuary.org.uk/what-we-do/knowledge-and-advice/for-owners/understanding-donkey-behaviour

75 Interesting World War I Facts | FactRetriever.com

https://thegraphicsfairy.com/19th-century-french-architecture/

https://www.nytimes.com/2022/09/21/realestate/housing-market-france-bergerac.html

https://www.manege1913paris.com/

https://en.wikipedia.org/wiki/Notre-Dame_de_Paris

https://www.discoverfrance.net/France/Paris/Monuments-Paris/Eiffel.shtml

https://museum.archives.gov/featured-document-display-honoring-native-american-soldiers-world-war-i-service

Featured Document Display: Honoring Native American Soldiers' World War I Service | National Archives Museum

https://www.history.com/topics/world-war-i/battle-of-gallipoli-1

information about Private Calvin Atchavit in France on Sept. 12, 1918,

https://www.ncbi.nlm.nih.gov/pmc/articles/PMC3052731/#:~:text=The%20
injured%20were%20carried%20through,behind%20the%20line%20of%20e
ntrenchment.

https://www.bl.uk/world-war-one/articles/wounding-in-world-war-one

https://www.ncbi.nlm.nih.gov/pmc/articles/PMC546312/#:~:text=For%20th
e%20most%20part%2C%20broken,to%20the%20sufferer%2C%20for%20e
ver.

https://www.ncbi.nlm.nih.gov/pmc/articles/PMC4523509/

https://www.npr.org/2016/12/29/505271148/descendants-of-native-
american-slaves-in-new-mexico-emerge-from-
obscurity#:~:text=In%20the%2018th%20and%2019th,assimilated%20into
%20New%20Mexican%20society.

As a husband-and-wife team, equally adding their individual perspectives and imagination. Authors **Amaia Joy and Geoffrey Carroll** tell a story that evokes you to take a vicarious trip in layered compelling writing, rich with a literary vision.

Amaia has lived in New Mexico her entire life as a cowgirl roving throughout the high deserts and mountains. She can brand a calf, shoot to kill a rattlesnake and ride a horse with ease. Amaia has lived the life of Annie-Oakley on the wide-open spaces, howled with the coyotes in the high mountains, hunted wild game along the Rio Grande. Amaia Joy holds the honor of being awarded the Distinguished Governors Award for Outstanding Women of New Mexico.

Geoffrey is an honored disabled Vet, a true American—Vietnam Veteran, 1st Air Mobile CAV artillery assigned to an infantry company as their Recon Sergent. He has been recognized for his heroism, fortitude, and valor, and is a recipient of many Vietnam Service Medals and Meritorious Citations. Geoffrey inspires the story with his reflections and experiences as a Soldier.

Amaia and Geoffrey both love and honor the Native American cultures and the Pueblo People of New Mexico. They know the individuals and places, and have lived the history amongst the many colorful traditions of New Mexico.

Amaia and Geoffrey love history and feel too many untold stories need to be revealed and shared. They will fill your hearts and minds with their splendid and layered contemporary fiction leaving lasting imprints on your souls.